The Truth About Ramsey Cain

He kissed her, and kissed her more, until he realized exactly what he was doing. As gracefully as he could without throwing himself across the room, he released his hold on her wondrously soft mouth and held her away from him.

After an eternity, she blinked her wide, blue eyes and brought her fingers to her lips.

"Perhaps you *should* be afraid of me." It was a statement spoken just above a whisper.

"Do I have reason to be?"

Ramsey backed away as though she had burned him. And she might have done just that. His entire body felt feverish and, like the chills that come with a fever, cold as ice.

He turned to the window. For a long moment she stood beside him in the silent office, while he willed himself to breathe, hoping to clear his head.

"I think, in the future, you should ignore Eberhart," he said, his voice perfectly controlled. "Now if you'll excuse me; I have calls to make this morning."

It was a dismissal, and if Landis followed her instincts and ran for the door, he wondered if she would ever be able to face him again.

What They Are Saying About
The Truth About Ramsey Cain

"A mysterious death, a Gothic mansion, and a brooding hero to die for.... for thrills, chills, and passion Marcy Graham-Waldenville delivers!"

S. K. McClafferty, author of
AS NIGHT FALLS

Wings

The Truth
About Ramsey Cain

by

Marcy Graham-Waldenville

A Wings ePress, Inc.

Contemporary Romance Novel

Wings ePress, Inc.

Edited by: Margery Casares
Copy Edited by: Elizabeth Burton
Senior Editor: Pat Casey
Managing Editor Kate Strong
Executive Editor: Lorraine Stephens
Cover Artist: Michelle Phelps

Wings ePress Books
http://www.wings-press.com

Copyright © 2002 by Marcy Graham-Waldenville
ISBN 1-59088-927-4

Published In the United States Of America

May 2002

Wings ePress Inc.
P. O. Box 38
Richmond, KY 40476-0038

Dedication

Dedicated to the memory of
my mother,
Elaine (Baker) Graham,

and my mother-in-law,
Emma (Coke) Waldenville.

Two woman
who taught me
the most important lessons
about love.

Prologue

In her tiny cubby-hole of an office, Landis Delaney slammed the dossier she carried onto her cluttered desk and paced the six feet to the wall and back.

Ramsey Cain!

Even the man's name gave her chills.

Suppressing a shiver, Landis scooped the file off the desk and sent it sailing in the general direction of the door.

"Whoa!" Melba Jackson poked her head around the door jam. "Is it safe to come in?"

Landis gave her a dubious look. "I won't promise anything."

Melba crouched to gather the dossier scattered over the floor." You know you've been ready for this move to undercover work for a long time. You can do this job with your eyes closed."

That her assistant already knew about the assignment didn't surprise Landis in the least. Melba, usually ahead of the game, had become invaluable over the last three years—for that very reason.

Three years! Landis had worked her butt off in the research department at WALH, Channel Seven, and for the last eighteen months she had headed research for the show *Pittsburgh Undercover*. Now all that hung by a thread, thanks to the show's anchorwoman, Paula Rice. Paula's endless ambition, and the fact that the producer practically lived in her pocket, had put Landis squarely behind the eight ball.

Landis sighed and dropped into her chair. "I know I can do the job. It isn't the assignment...well, it *is* the assignment *and* the crappy way she sprang it on me. I really don't want to get within ten feet of that...wife killer."

Melba peeked over the end of the desk. "Then don't take the assignment."

Landis snorted. "She found a clause in my contract. If I say no she goes to legal and tells them I'm not living up to my contract. One bad report from her and my whole career goes down in flames. And if I'm out there's no guarantee the next head of research won't bring in his own assistant. You'll be out of a job, too. And even if they don't fire you, there are *not* a lot of department heads who let their assistant go home early to take her kids to the zoo."

"You don't have to remind me." Melba sighed. "So, what do we do?"

"You have to stay in close touch with me in case I need help. I have to go to Cherry Run." Landis threw up her hands. "I have to pretend I'm Ramsey Cain's new personal assistant, live under that same roof with him, get him to trust me, then find out if he really threw his wife down the stairs for the insurance money. Oh, yes, and not get myself killed in the process."

"What Paula really wants is for you to find proof positive that Ramsey Cain killed his wife. You could always find out that he's innocent, you know. There are a lot of people who think he didn't kill his wife."

"Easy for you to say. You'll be safe in the city with only random acts of senseless violence to worry about. I'll be living under the same roof with an uptown Bluebeard."

"A *gorgeous* uptown Bluebeard," Melba said, holding out a photo of Ramsey Cain that had fallen from the folder.

"Yeah." Landis looked at the grainy snapshot. He *was* a handsome, dark and mysterious man. The kind of man most women would give their eyeteeth to call their own. But Holly Richards Cain had given a lot more than that. She had given her life.

It was a full minute before Landis shuffled the photo back into the file. She put her hand over her stomach to steady the sinking feeling there. "I'm sure I don't care what he looks like."

One

Landis Delaney stopped her car in front of the great house perched high on the tree-shrouded hill. The dark windows of the mansion stared at her, and she couldn't stop the nervous chill that coursed through her body.

She studied the place known as Kinross House. The formal, elegant Georgian mansion seemed very out of place in the small mining community. But the years had been kind to the grand old dame of Cherry Run, Pennsylvania, kinder than they had been to Landis.

Why are you doing this? she asked herself.

That was simple. She had no choice. Her bosses at *Pittsburgh Undercover* had used a tiny clause in what she thought was an ironclad contract as researcher to force her into this hideous position. She could either take the undercover assignment or lose the career she had worked so hard for.

Each argument she had used to get out of it had been turned around on her by the show's anchorwoman, Paula Rice, until the station manager finally sided with Rice and sent Landis back to her hometown to find out what a cold-blooded killer ate for breakfast. She just hoped it wasn't an indentured researcher.

She was now Ramsey Cain's new executive assistant, and she had been told that Cain was very impressed with her fictional resume. Bill Gaiser, corporate headhunter and general sleazeball, had told Paula that Cain was searching for a secretary and had, at Paula's insistence, offered up Landis Delaney as the only applicant. The worm had taken hundreds of dollars from Cain to find the perfect secretary and had taken thousands from Paula for his cooperation and silence.

Landis crawled out onto the flagstone walkway. Her mind began an unwanted review of the story of Ramsey Cain's wife's death.

Despite some people's belief that the man was innocent, Landis was convinced Cain was guilty as sin, and the thought of standing face-to-face with a man who could kill his wife and coolly lie about it turned her stomach. To her, he was nothing more than a very lucky killer.

But somewhere deep inside Landis had to admit she was also hellishly curious about Ramsey Cain. An occupational hazard, she told herself. News researchers can't stand *not* having all the answers. And too much of Cain's story just didn't add up.

He'd been born the only son of a wealthy coal mine operator in Cherry Run, Pennsylvania, a small town of less than two thousand souls. He had attended Carnegie-Mellon University and, after graduation, had begun a successful architectural firm. Within a relatively short ten years it had grown into the tri-state area's premier developer. During that time, Cain married his college sweetheart, Holly Richards. The couple was the darling of Pittsburgh's social life.

They moved from the upscale neighborhood of Fox Chapel to the family home in Cherry Run, and Cain spent his time commuting between the city and home. Then, one night in late July three years before, Holly Richards Cain fell—or was thrown—from the top of the staircase to her death.

Landis got her purse and briefcase out of the car. She took her time, gathering her courage. She tried to stop the information overload. It was no use. Like a tap left on, the things she had learned about Ramsey Cain poured through her mind.

She remembered that very early in the investigation Cain was suspected of murdering his beautiful wife. Talk of multimillion dollar insurance payoffs and illicit lovers had only fueled the fire of public opinion that burned for answers. *Pittsburgh Undercover* and Paula Rice had been there to fan the flames, offering nightly reports on the investigation and the coroner's inquest. In the end, the high level of alcohol in the victim's blood was blamed for her death. According to the autopsy, aside from the sorts of bruises and contusions one would expect to find after such a severe fall, there were no unexplained wounds, no blunt-force trauma, no strangulation. The fact there had never been a hint of scandal prior to that night, no 911 calls or reports of abuse, led the Allegheny County Coroner's Office to rule Holly Richards Cain's death an accident.

Speculation had not died so quickly. Ramsey Cain became a sort of macabre celebrity. His every move was reported and dissected for public consumption, courtesy of Paula Rice—until one day he had simply vanished. Reporters, Paula included, had tried to reach him at his house in Cherry Run and had even camped on his front lawn for weeks on end.

Slowly, interest died away and his name stopped showing up in every newspaper. But no one knew how the wealthy recluse spent his days, or with whom he spent his nights.

Now, it was up to Landis to find out.

She paused on the sidewalk, put her purse over her arm and shifted her briefcase, then glanced at the dark Palladian window on the second floor of the west wing addition. She had the distinct impression that someone or something watched her.

The catch on the gate squeaked when she swung it open, and made her shiver. Squaring her shoulders, Landis walked toward the house. The bad feeling grew stronger with each step she took. It was as if the house itself didn't want her to come any closer.

But she did, putting one determined foot in front of the other, until she paused on the stoop outside the wide double doors.

"Congratulations, Landis, you made it," she whispered, pressing the doorbell. "And you gave yourself the creeps."

The door opened. Instantly, her breath caught in her throat. The doorway filled with the tallest, ugliest woman Landis had ever seen in her life.

Mrs. Lurch. Landis couldn't push the unkind thought out of her mind as she looked up into that hard face.

The woman looked to be in her late fifties and stood at least six inches above Landis's own five-foot-nine. Her navy-blue dress clung to her narrow frame like a bad set of curtains, and a thick steel-gray braid hung down her back. "Good morning," she said in a perfect baritone that, oddly enough, fit her. "You must be Miss Delaney."

"Landis," Landis said.

"My name is Alice Eberhart; I'm the housekeeper. Mr. Cain will join you in the library." The older woman spoke without the hint of a smile.

Landis made a mental note: *friendly in a frightening sort of way*, then followed Mrs. Alice Eberhart into the dimly-lit foyer.

Landis took in the old house's interior: the high ceilings with their distinctive crown molding; the deep patina of the hardwood floor; the small touches that maintained the house's air of age and quality despite the new addition of the west wing.

As a child, Landis had passed Kinross House every day in the school bus and knew the history of the place. She knew that Ramsey Cain's great-grandfather, Duncan Cain, the founder of Bitter Clay Coal Mines, had built the great house for his family and named it for the small town in Scotland where he had been born. She knew, too, that old Duncan's fortune had been made off the sweat of the miners, who had struggled to keep body and soul together in the poorly constructed shacks that dotted the valley below.

Her father and grandfather had mined coal for the Bitter Clay Mining Company. Landis had heard the story more often than fairy tales as she grew up. The idea that she somehow betrayed her working-class roots gnawed at her as she followed the housekeeper into the expensively furnished library.

Landis took a seat on one of the leather chairs that faced the cherry desk. She would now be working, even if only in a backhanded sort of way, for one of those men her Grandpa Delaney had called '*capitalist leeches, heartless, money-grubbing...*'

"Good morning. I'm Ramsey Cain."

His voice filled the room and rumbled through Landis, leaving a trail of pure energy in its wake. She turned slightly to watch him enter the library, and every coherent thought deserted her. This was her Bluebeard? He was more like a Greek God.

The man moving silently across the room didn't resemble at all the man she had seen in news clips coming out of a coroner's office, a vacant stare haunting his eyes. Hair the color of black coffee that had been neatly trimmed three years ago now swung in silken ripples around broad shoulders as he moved. His eyes, a bottomless and penetrating gray, gazed deeply into her own. Self-imposed exile had been *very* good to Ramsey Cain.

Devastating good looks aside, something about him still made Landis uneasy. This was Ramsey Cain, uptown Bluebeard...a wife killer. That she had to remind herself of that fact made her *very* uneasy.

"Landis Delaney, sir," the housekeeper announced.

"Thank you, Eberhart," he said, and what was left of Landis's logical mind noted that he addressed the housekeeper by only her surname. That, like her voice, suited her.

He didn't take a seat behind the desk, which would have been a nice, safe distance. Instead, he picked up what must have been her false resume, circled the desk and sat on its polished surface, directly in front of her. He was so close she could smell the soft scent of his cologne and had to look up, because one powerfully muscled thigh was in her direct line of vision.

"Why do you want to work here?" The coldness in that awe-inspiring voice caught Landis off-guard as much as the question.

"I guess because..." she faltered. She didn't want to work here. She didn't want to sit in this expensive leather chair and be stared at by the coldest eyes she'd ever seen. And she didn't like having to come up with spur-of-the-moment lies. It wreaked havoc on her orderly mind. "I got tired of being stabbed in the back for doing a good job, and of women with smaller brains and bigger bras getting promoted over me. You don't have an office. You'll just have me. And...I...like your insurance package."

He hesitated a moment, then glanced at the resume in front of him. "Do you always talk so fast?"

Landis opened her mouth to tell him that she only did it when she was nervous, but Cain turned that deep, chilling gaze her way again, and she thought better of it. "No."

She also thought about Holly Richards. This man had been her husband, had eaten breakfast with her and talked to her about work, had slept with that thick, sable mane on the pillow next to her.

And—Landis forced herself to add—he had tossed her down the stairs.

"Your references are impeccable," he said, jolting her away from her morose daydream. He ran a hand through his hair, pushing it back from his face.

She mumbled a *thank you* and took advantage of the time he spent studying the fake resume to study him.

He wore black trousers and a black band-collar dress shirt that he had buttoned to the throat. She could see the well-formed muscles of his shoulders, arms and chest beneath the light cotton.

He would be amazing in a T-shirt and jeans, with all that hair slipping forward over his dark brows.

He looked down at her, and Landis tensed. She knew what would come next, and she scrambled to remember everything she had been told to say.

"Jerry Smith at Northeastern Mutual Insurance mentions here that he hated to have you leave."

How in the world could she concentrate on her assortment of lies when he watched her like that? Jerry who? Oh, yes, fictitious ex-boss.

"Office politics...is that the only reason you left?" he asked.

"I was a victim of downsizing." She flinched at the choice of the word "victim," but Ramsey Cain continued to watch her, his face unreadable. "Northeastern decided to cut back on the office in Kittanning, and they let seven secretaries go." Yes! She recited the lie exactly the way she had practiced. But she suddenly wasn't sure whether to be proud of herself or not.

"With your background, I can't believe you would have trouble finding another job."

"Thank you." This lying thing was getting easier.

"And you have no qualms about working for me?"

Was that another strange question meant to throw her off, or was she just getting paranoid?

She was surprised to see something flicker in his profound gray eyes. That question had come from somewhere deeply hidden. Then just as quickly as the chink in his armor appeared it vanished, leaving Landis to wonder if she had imagined that flash of vulnerability. A carefully constructed wall rose up between them.

Did she have any misgivings about working for him?

Mustering all her courage, she looked him in the face and told the biggest lie of all. "None."

His voice left a trail of wreckage along her nervous system. He was intelligent, strong. For one brief moment there had been something painfully honest in his dark gaze. And, as long as she was being honest with herself, she liked the faint worry lines that crisscrossed his forehead.

She reminded herself again who he was by mentally ticking off a few facts of his wife's death. She looked up into the hard lines of his face and suppressed a shiver. Was she looking into the face of a cold-blooded killer?

Landis had been born with a researcher's mind, able to gather the facts, sort out the rumor and gossip and make a decision. Once she did that, she never, ever, went back, and only changed her opinion when she had proved beyond a shadow of a doubt that some of the facts were in error or missing. She didn't get gut feelings, and she didn't follow the sort of intuition that got most people into trouble.

So, what was this nagging little voice in her head that pointed out the breadth of his shoulders and the elegance in his strong fingers? And why did it tell her she needed to look at the evidence of Holly's death again.

One corner of Ramsey's mouth quirked upward in what might have been a smile, had there been any warmth in it. The effect was both chilling and exciting.

"Will I be working in this room?" she asked, glancing around the huge library for anything to look at other than him.

"No," he said, coming to his feet suddenly. "I have an office on the second floor. I'll show you to your bedroom first. And later let you get familiar with the set-up."

A shiver snaked its way down her back. She didn't want to have him show her into her bedroom, or where she could put her shampoo and toothbrush. Where was the housekeeper? Wasn't this her job? The very idea of being in a bedroom with this dangerous, sexy man sent her internal warning system into meltdown.

But there wasn't any way out of it, so she rose from her chair and followed Cain out the library door.

Landis glanced up the wide stairs. The bannister gleamed in the soft light from the blown-glass chandelier that hung above the foyer. Cain's Italian shoes made a muffled sound on the rubber runner that protected the antique rose-print carpet.

As she headed toward the steps, the thought struck her. This was where Holly Cain had met her death! These had to be the stairs she tumbled down that fateful night.

"Is something wrong?" he asked as he led the way up the long staircase.

"No...nothing." Landis said, telling herself she had to get better at hiding her nervousness.

He came to an abrupt stop, one foot on the landing, and turned his dark head to stare at her. His face was inscrutable. "Never feel that you can't be honest with me, Landis," he said. Turning, he resumed his steady climb to the second floor.

The sound of her name, spoken in that deep, resonant voice, had the effect of a ricocheting bullet in her head, and his words battered against her conscience. She muttered something in reply and, through sheer dint of will, managed to follow Ramsey Cain up the stairs.

~ * ~

Ramsey was conscious of the sound of his new assistant's footfalls on the old carpet and the scent of vanilla and musk that clung to her. Too conscious, he thought. He paused at the top of the stairs and waited for her to catch up.

A little voice inside his head told him not to take her to that room, to give her any room but the one adjacent to his office.

It had the most amenities and was the most recently remodeled, he argued with himself.

You're tempting fate, that little voice warned.

It has its own bathroom, he thought.

It was intended to be Holly's bedroom, it countered.

And she's dead, he thought, stilling his nagging conscience.

The room really was lovely. He'd had it extensively redone just before Holly's death. The furniture was a collection of his mother's favorite pieces: top quality, understated and elegant. The evening light filled the room with a warm golden glow, and a soft breeze from the woods provided an earthy perfume. It was just the sort of room he would have designed for someone like Landis Delaney if given the chance.

The fact that he had designed it for his late wife, hoping it would satisfy her, meant nothing. Holly had hated it, called it dull and refused to move her things from the guestroom she had occupied since the move from the city. But Ramsey had known the real reason Holly hated the room. It was too close to his bedroom and she had hated him with a passion.

It had never truly been Holly's room, he reasoned with himself. It was just another guestroom. And the fact it was connected to the office through an adjoining door made it the logical choice for his assistant.

Ramsey looked down at Landis before opening the door.

Dear God, but she was lovely. From the scattering of freckles on her slightly turned-up nose to the shapely legs that stretched from the hem of her short business suit to her comfortably low pumps she was every inch a thoroughly desirable female. The kind of woman who made teenage boys groan and construction workers whistle. The sort of secretary that distracted her boss while she took perfect dictation, typed a phenomenal number of words per minute and ran the office with the efficiency of a drill sergeant. At least he hoped she was that type of secretary.

She smiled and Ramsey's chest tightened. How could he drag this unsuspecting woman into his life?

But he had known he would the moment he entered his dreary library and saw her there. And later, when she gave him that nervous smile, as she did now, his heart had slammed into his ribs and he knew her fate was sealed.

With her small, heart-shaped face and wide, intelligent blue eyes, she was like a beacon of light that drew him toward her. Her very presence filled the dark rooms of his house with warmth, and he desperately needed that warmth.

He made her uncomfortable; he knew that, too, the moment he walked into the library. And though she was open and honest during their brief interview; she tactfully sidestepped every opportunity he had given her to ask about his past.

Did she know about his past?

Of course. His face and the police reports of Holly's death had been front-page news and that sleazy tabloid television show had harped on it for months. That moment, when she had hesitated on the stairs, said everything she had been too polite or too afraid to say out loud.

Images of that night three years ago still haunted him. Now, he wondered if that look of doubt in Landis Delaney's eyes would haunt him as well?

Ramsey opened the door and stepped into the room. Landis followed, watching her new boss adjust the setting on the thermostat and noticing the scowl that tainted his handsome features.

"Someone has the air conditioning set too low. It'll warm up in here in no time," Ramsey said moving though the room.

He looked oddly out of place amid the delicate furnishings.

"Well, at least I know it works," Landis said, feigning a cheerfulness she didn't feel.

Ramsey opened a narrow door and stepped into the small bath. He checked the water faucet in the bathtub and glanced in the closet.

"I have two suitcases in my car," she said.

"I'll bring them up to you and move your car into the drive if you'll give me the keys."

Crossing the room in long strides, he stopped next to her at the foot of the bed.

He was so tall, and the dark hair framing his face and shoulders added an air of intimidation to his already overwhelming presence.

He held out a hand and Landis found herself staring at it. It was well-proportioned. His fingers were long and tapered...elegant...strong, certainly strong enough to overpower any woman and—

"Landis?" His voice commanded her attention.

What did he want? Oh, yes...the keys. She reached into her pocket and found them, then dropped them into his hand.

"Don't worry. I *will* return them," he said pointedly. "If you need anything call Eberhart on the intercom—she's button number four."

Cain reached out and brushed one of his elegant hands over her bare arm, perhaps to try to convey some of his body heat, perhaps because Landis had silently wondered what his touch would feel like.

The brief contact filled her with a warmth that drove the chill from her limbs. There was something in that touch, something too intense. But he said nothing, only turned and left the room, closing the door behind him.

A trace of doubt began to gnaw at her.

The media had been the source of her opinion that Ramsey Cain was a cruel killer. But she, better than anyone, knew what made the people who created those headlines tick. Scandal produces ratings! Her presence in this house proved that nothing was too low for the likes of Paula Rice.

What if popular opinion had been wrong? And if it was, how could she do what Paula expected of her? How could she be a part of his destruction again?

Two

Later, despite promising herself she would not start at every sound, a knock on her door made Landis jump.

"It's Eberhart, miss," that strange, baritone voice called. "I have your suitcases."

Landis opened the door and found the housekeeper looking wearily down at her.

"Mr. Cain moved your car into the drive," Eberhart said, holding out Landis's keys.

Landis took the keys from the woman's oversized hands. "Why you're just a Jill-of-all-trades," she remarked with a smile that faded quickly when the other woman only stared at her.

"I beg your pardon?" Eberhart said icily.

"Never mind. Thanks." Landis pocketed the keys.

"It's my job," the woman said without returning Landis's smile. "Will there be anything else?"

"Would you mind answering a question?"

The housekeeper gave her a thoughtful look, then nodded her head.

"Is Mr. Cain a good boss?" Landis asked, trying to look casual by opening one of the suitcases.

"He's very considerate."

"I mean, is he easy to get along with?"

"Mr. Cain and I have never had any difficulties," Eberhart's eyes narrowed. "Are you concerned that you will not get along with him?"

"No...it's just," Landis stammered, not certain what to say next. "There was so much talk..."

"One can't believe everything one hears," Eberhart said coolly. "Rumors abound and are often erroneous."

The very subject she had been trying to get to fell right into her lap. "You mean the rumors about *Mrs.* Cain? You don't believe Mr. Cain had anything to do with his wife's death?" Landis asked in a whisper.

"I believe it has nothing to do with my work—or with yours." Eberhart started for the door.

"In other words, don't ask," Landis said.

"It would be the smart thing to do. You don't strike me as a stupid girl."

Was that supposed to be a compliment?

"Thank you...I think. One more thing," Landis said, stopping her. "Where is Mr. Cain's office?"

"Right through there," Eberhart said, pointing to the door on the wall opposite Landis's bed.

"You mean my room is connected to the office?" But when she turned to question the housekeeper, she saw the door closing.

Landis took a deep breath and tapped lightly on the office door, but only silence came from the other side. After a long pause, she opened the door.

It was the office all right, paneled in honey pine and filled with everything the modern American businessman needed to run an empire from the comfort of his own home.

A set of wide double doors dominated the opposite wall. Where did they lead? she wondered. A third door centered on the wall to the left and led back to the hallway.

In the center of the room a large drafting table cluttered with blueprints sat like an island in a sea of confusion. A desk sat in one corner between filing cabinets. Untidy piles cluttered every inch of the room. A computer hummed on the desk. Afternoon sunlight filtered in from two tall windows on the west wall.

Landis crossed the room and looked out the windows into the front yard. They were the windows that had made her feel as though someone watched her as she approached the house. Had he been standing there watching her?

She shook off a chill and turned her attention back to the room. Opening a file cabinet she looked over the most jumbled filing system she had ever seen.

The double doors swung open and Ramsey Cain stepped into the room. "Landis," he said, obviously as surprised to find her there as she was to be caught rifling the files.

"I was...anxious to get started." She hated to stammer in front of him but for some reason she couldn't seem to stop herself.

A sheet of paper got caught in the drawer when she tried to close it, pulling the entire pile to the floor. Landis knelt to pick them up. "Did I mention I'm a klutz?" she asked. She reached up to steady a second teetering stack and felt a warm hand cover her own.

"So I see."

He stood over her, and she realized her hand trembled under his. His gaze slide over her, and her heart clutched painfully in her chest.

If eyes were a mirror of the soul, then his soul was troubled. In the deep gray depths she saw a flash of emotion his stony expression did nothing to betray. An unexpected pang of guilt washed over her. It was her job to discover the mysteries lurking behind those eyes.

Ramsey took the papers from her hand and stacked them with the other clutter on the desk. "I was coming to get you."

Landis did her best not to think of what *coming to get you* could have meant.

"Eberhart told me where to find the office," she said, catching another pile before it toppled. "This is a very...convenient...floor plan."

"I suppose you see why I need a good assistant?" He stalked to the drafting table. "The last year has been...difficult."

A flicker of pain crossed his face, a look that gave the illusion of momentary vulnerability. He brushed his long hair behind his shoulder and Landis noticed the marks on his neck. Three pale ribbons against his darker skin that started beneath his ear and stopped over his jugular vein.

Ramsey had claimed at the time of his wife's death that during an argument Holly had attempted to slap him. He had deflected the attack and she'd stumbled. Police had speculated that perhaps Mrs. Cain had scratched her husband as he attempted to throw her down the stairs.

"You have an unnerving habit of staring," he said, breaking into her thoughts.

"I...don't think I can straighten this out in a day." She pointedly ignored his comment about staring, but her gaze shifted from his eyes to his neck.

He touched the scars with his fingertips. "I don't expect you to perform miracles."

"Maybe we should discuss what it is you *do* expect."

"I expect you to take care of the office. Typing, keying files into that damned computer. You'll keep up with the office in Pittsburgh and take care of all professional correspondence."

"And personal?" she asked without thinking.

"I have no personal correspondence. But if I need anything *personal* that, too, would be your duty."

Landis fought a blush.

He turned to face her and his expression made her forget the innuendo. There was something in his eyes that resembled...desperation. "More important, I expect you to keep me from making mistakes."

Landis thought that a joke, and gave a short laugh that died as she watched his face darken.

"I've made costly mistakes. I expect you to keep me from making more."

The intensity in his face turned Landis's mouth dry. She wet her lips with the tip of her tongue. "What kind of mistakes?"

"Missed meetings, forgotten appointments, lost date books. I've been...distracted. I want you to keep the distraction from affecting my business." He watched her with those fathomless eyes.

She wasn't actually here to be a real help to him, and the thought that this man would be depending on her, only to be betrayed, made her ill.

"I'll do my best." She hoped her voice didn't give away the guilt burning in her throat.

~ * ~

The emotions Ramsey read in Landis' eyes amazed him. Doubt, fear and something else he couldn't name flickered behind her intense blue gaze. He had the oddest desire to draw her into his arms and tell her the marks on his neck were nothing—that he was neither a killer nor a madman. But he couldn't, because he wasn't sure what he was.

She tried to look nonchalant but couldn't quite pull it off. He made her nervous, and he knew it.

"I think I have everything I need," she said, turning her attention to the computer.

"Good," he answered, relieved that their conversation was over. "I'll go talk to Mrs. McCreary about dinner. We eat at seven. You'll join us, of course."

She gave him a smile and his chest tightened.

"Seven," she repeated. "Should I dress?"

He fought the urge to laugh. "Just wear something comfortable."

"Mr. Cain. One more thing." She stopped him before he left and pointed to the double doors. "Where do those doors lead?"

He paused and fought to keep amusement from his voice. "Please, you must call me Ramsey. And that is *my* bedroom."

~ * ~

As the only remaining member of Ramsey's family, the opinion of his aunt, Orphia Salankewietz, would be important to her nephew, so Landis decided she needed to make a good impression on the woman.

She crossed the foyer at precisely seven o'clock and heard nothing in the large dinning room—no voices, no familial chatter. It was as if the two people sharing the table were strangers eating in a restaurant.

A tremor of anxiety coursed through her. Ramsey Cain had bought her secretary act, but what about his aunt? Landis reminded herself she had no choice—she would win Ramsey's aunt over because she had to.

Ramsey stood as she entered, and Landis's carefully nurtured calm left her in a rush. He had dressed in black trousers, a white shirt similar to the one he'd worn earlier buttoned to the band-collar. Over the shirt he wore a beautiful vest striped in varying shades of gray.

It was stark and it suited him, but she had the impression it was more a suit of armor than one of fine Italian wool. It insulated him from the world. Still, as he walked across the room to escort her to her seat, she had to admit he was devastatingly handsome.

"Good evening," he said, taking her arm in an outdated gesture. Landis felt the muscles in his forearm work beneath the crisp cotton of his shirt. She told herself not to react to the strength in that arm and not to think what that strength might be capable of.

She glanced at the elderly woman who occupied a place at the foot of the mahogany table. She was small, with an elf-like face that had been creased by time, and she watched Landis with sharp eyes.

"This is Orphia Salankewietz, my aunt," Ramsey said. "Aunt Orphy, this is Landis Delaney, my new assistant."

"What kind of name is 'Landis?'" the old woman asked in a voice that sounded like a rusted chainsaw.

"It's a nice name," Ramsey said, taking his seat at the head of the table.

"Dear God!" Orphy cried, her hand flying to her throat. "Is she mute?"

"Of course not," Ramsey sighed.

"Then let her speak for herself." Ramsey's aunt fixed Landis with a smile.

"I'm pleased to meet you, Mrs. Salankewietz." Landis said.

The old woman presented her with a toothy grin. "Please, call me Orphy."

Eberhart set a plate of salad in front of Landis, who muttered a thank-you.

"Where are you from, dear?" Orphy asked, moving the contents of her plate around as though she must inspect it.

Landis had to decide how much of her past she wanted to divulge. She took a deep breath and tried a little of the truth. "Here, in Armstrong County."

"Not Cherry Run, surely," Orphy protested. "Did you say 'Delaney?'"

"Yes," Landis didn't volunteer any more information.

Ramsey cleared his throat, catching his aunt's attention, and warned her off the interrogation with a stern stare.

"If she is to live here, I would like to know who she is, who her people are." Orphy said defiantly.

"I was born in the old Kittanning hospital. I graduated from Cherry Run High School. I've never been arrested nor had any kind of run-in with the law. I pay my taxes on time but never early, and I was baptized a Lutheran but I haven't been to church in years."

Orphy gave her that animated smile. "I like her, Ramsey. Is she staying?"

"If you don't scare her off," Ramsey said, glancing at Landis as he opened his napkin in his lap.

"I believe your taste in women is getting better," Orphy said, digging into her salad.

Eberhart rattled the meat platter, drawing a glare from the old woman.

"Of course," Orphy added, "the last woman you dragged home wasn't an honest working girl. She had higher aspirations."

"Aunt Orphy," Ramsey warned quietly.

Eberhart set the platter of roast beef down with a bang. Landis noticed a look that passed between the housekeeper and Ramsey's aunt and wondered what was behind those glares and why the old woman had been able to niggle the housekeeper by casting aspersions on the late Mrs. Cain. There had to be a *story* behind those looks.

Landis also noticed she had begun to think like a reporter and suppressed a shudder of revulsion.

"I knew some Delaneys once," Orphy said suddenly. "Or maybe Maury knew them."

"I'll bet that was it," Cain said, then turned his attention to Landis. "Aunt Orphy gets...confused."

Landis understood immediately, and apparently so did his aunt.

"But she's not deaf," the old woman added. "Or stupid."

~ * ~

Ramsey pushed his plate away with a sigh and motioned for Eberhart to bring him a drink. He'd had enough of acting the good host, and he had no appetite for either the food or the pretense.

"Would you care to join me, Landis?" he asked, indicating the decanter of whiskey Eberhart placed in front of him.

"No, thank you."

He focused on the glass the housekeeper offered. "It's my only indulgence."

"More's the pity," Orphy said with a sarcastic laugh.

He ignored the pointed comment. His aunt had been after him for months to end his exile, but, then, the dear old soul didn't understand his need for penance.

"Ramsey thinks because one woman broke his heart it doesn't work anymore," Orphy said, picking at her dinner. "He's stubborn, like his mother, God rest her soul."

Ramsey stopped listening, but continued watching Landis closely, not just because she was beautiful or because of the way her dress hugged her soft curves or the way light from the chandelier danced on her shining curls. She was interesting, and, oddly enough, she seemed to be enjoying herself even if she wasn't sure what to make of him...or his lovably eccentric aunt.

He couldn't blame her for not understanding them. They were a dismal lot. Orphy had done her best to make Landis comfortable but over-did it, as usual. Eberhart rattled the china as though she might send the next plate into someone's lap, and he had run out of polite conversation shortly after "Good evening."

None of it flustered Miss Delaney, though. She nibbled the apple pie Eberhart served for dessert, smiling, answering Orphy's endless questions. His aunt enjoyed their talk, but Aunt Orphy liked everyone who wasn't pretentious.

That had been only one of the many things his aunt had hated about Holly. Holly had pleaded with Ramsey to move his aunt into a home for the elderly. When that didn't work Holly became sullen. She took his aunt's often outlandish comments as personal attacks and resented the slightest remark.

Finally, Orphy had decided it would be better if she spent the winter with friends in Georgia. He tensed at the memory and drained the glass of whiskey.

Holly had treated Orphy's departure as a victory. But Ramsey often wondered—if his aunt had been home that night, would Holly still be alive? No one had been around. The fight had become more vicious, more out of control than usual, until...

"Ramsey?" Orphy asked sharply, drawing him from his morbid memories. She scowled, but it was Landis and her cool blue stare that made him twist uncomfortably in his chair.

"You see what I mean, my dear. Off in a world of his own," Orphy chided softly.

That was it. He had reached his limit. "I think this day has been long enough. Breakfast is at seven o'clock," he said for Landis's benefit.

~ * ~

Landis had watched him watching her and saw his face grow darker with each passing moment. She worried she had said something to upset him, but she hadn't expected such an abrupt dismissal.

"Will you need anything else tonight?" Ramsey asked.

His voice made her forget what she'd been thinking.

"I'll be fine." She turned to Eberhart to thank her for everything, but the housekeeper's expression made the *thank you* lodge in Landis's throat.

Eberhart's brows furrowed above eyes that swept Landis with a hard stare, and her mouth twisted down in the corners in a tight bow of disapproval. Her normal expression soon returned, but Landis was left rattled to the bone. What was it about this house, about these people, that made her feel as if she'd fallen through the looking glass?

"I'm going to bed, too," Orphy announced, springing to her feet with an agility that belied her seventy-odd years. She stopped next to her nephew and affectionately patted his cheek. "Have a good night, my dear. I have bingo at eight in the morning, so try not to prowl on my end of the hall. Those big feet of yours make this old house creak."

~ * ~

Ramsey kissed his aunt's cheek and turned to watch Landis rise from her chair. He kept his hands clenched at his side. It was the only way he could be certain he wouldn't reach out to touch her. She was so sweet, so soft beneath her cautious exterior. That softness drew him to her.

"Good night, Mr. Cain," she said. Her skirt swished sensuously around her shapely legs as she slowly crossed the dinning room.

"I thought we decided you'd call me 'Ramsey?'" he said. He silently cursed himself. This time he couldn't convince himself he didn't know what might happen. This was worse than it had been with Holly. Far worse, because he knew what he was capable of and what it might cost Landis Delaney.

~ * ~

Landis saw the tension in Ramsey's shoulders. He would likely be greatly relieved when everyone departed, but still the look he fixed her with warmed her like a heated caress.

Through the evening—indeed, from the moment she first saw him—Ramsey Cain's glower, his sardonic charm and the dark past that swirled around him like smoke and brimstone had confused and frustrated her. Out of those feelings, fantasies began to spring. Landis had tried to stop them, to remind herself over and over who he was, who she was. But they came anyway. What had happened to her logic, to the clear mind that had made her such a good researcher? It was as though she had left that mind in Pittsburgh, as though it was something she'd forgotten to pack. And from the way things looked, it would get worse.

She blinked, praying the moment would pass, but Ramsey seemed content to hold her in his intense gaze. His jaw tensed slightly, the only movement in a face that could have been chiseled from stone.

She had to get herself under control, had to stop looking at this man as someone more than he was. He was just a strange, reclusive millionaire, one who might or might not have killed his wife.

"I hope this evening was not too uncomfortable?" he said, and despite her best efforts his deep voice filled her with warmth.

"I like your aunt very much. She's...entertaining." In the half-light she saw shadows in his stormy-gray eyes.

"Then you haven't changed your mind about working for me? I wanted to make your first night at Kinross House pleasant."

"I'm looking forward to working for you." Landis suddenly felt guilty and tore her gaze away. She didn't like what she was doing, didn't like lying to this guy. She felt trapped between this unnerving, sexy man and her own dismal lack of a future.

He smiled, a genuine smile that deepened the creases in his lean cheeks and chased the shadows from his eyes. Landis's breath stopped in her chest.

"I'm grateful," he said, but, to her disappointment, his smile slipped away. "Sleep well, Landis."

The evening had taken a toll on her. She desperately wanted to escape to her new room, to lose herself in the romance novel waiting on her nightstand, to forget Paula's threats and Orphy Salankewietz's friendly chatter. But mostly she wanted to get away from Ramsey Cain.

She glanced nervously at the foot of the stairs, at the spot where Holly Richards Cain's life had ended. She didn't want to think about that, either.

Distracted, Landis climbed the stairs.

"Is something wrong, Miss Delaney?" Eberhart's voice drifted down from the top of the stairs.

"I...didn't see you." Landis hesitated.

"I'd like a word with you, if I may?" the housekeeper said, then pursed her thin lips.

After a second to collect herself, Landis fixed her with a stony stare. "Actually, I was hoping to talk to you. What was the meaning of that look you gave me a few minutes ago?"

Eberhart folded her long, graceless fingers in a very prim pose and cleared her throat. "While you are living in this house it would be advisable for you to take your meals in the kitchen with the cook and myself."

Landis was too stunned to reply.

"It's very bad form for the staff to fraternize with the family, and I fear your...informality with Mr. Cain is out of place. Once you have gotten used to the way we do things—"

"Stop!" Landis snapped. "I think someone's been watching a little too much *Upstairs, Downstairs.* I don't work for you. I'm Mr. Cain's personal assistant, not a member of the household staff."

Eberhart said nothing.

"Is that all you wanted?" Landis asked, crossing her arms.

The older woman only nodded her gray head.

"Look. I don't want any hard feelings between us. It's just that we all have our own way of doing things. I tend to get involved with the people around me. It's a curse." Landis tried to smile, but the housekeeper's eyes grew cold and hard.

"In this house, it could be a deadly curse. Good night, Miss Delaney."

"Good night." Landis watched the housekeeper move silently down the hall before finding her own room. She closed her bedroom door and locked it. It would be difficult to set aside Cain's past and her overwhelming attraction to him in order to do all the things Paula expected of her. What was far worse, she now wanted to know Ramsey Cain's secrets not for Paula or for the good of the damn show. She wanted to know for herself.

His timeless eyes made her heart skip a beat, and his too-infrequent smile made her weak in the knees. Damn it, she didn't need this. She wasn't up for this two-bit 007 stuff. She was a bookworm, a researcher, far more comfortable with facts and figures than stormy-eyed men who oozed erotic charm. And she wasn't used to lying. At any moment she was certain all her secrets would tumble out, and she didn't want to think what would happen if that man found out he had been duped.

Three

Ramsey waited for the house to grow quiet, then poured himself another drink. He thought about his new assistant, and with the whiskey putting a fuzzy halo around everything it seemed as good a pastime as any.

Her soft skin, sensuous mouth and long legs had left him more than a little uncomfortable on his hard chair. He tried telling himself, physical attributes aside, he didn't know enough about her to form an acceptable opinion. And he had learned the hard way that the opposite sex was rarely what it appeared to be. Sometimes the best package held the worst present. And Landis Delaney had a great package.

He wanted her, more than he had wanted anyone in a very long time. How long had he known her? A few short hours, and here he was getting blissfully drunk and developing a first- class fantasy.

But, damn, it was good to feel something again. He shifted in his chair and tried to find a comfortable position for his uncomfortable physical state. He wasn't doing himself a favor. He really should think of something else.

Another mouthful of whiskey burned a path down his throat. The antique grandfather clock in the hall chimed the hour, and the automatic light clicked on in the foyer.

From his seat, he could see through the archway into the foyer, and he tried to focus his blurring vision on that cursed placed at the foot of the stairs. He didn't see Holly, but it was as though she were still there. It was as though her ghost had never left the house, as though she could materialize every now and then and leave him grappling with his anger and his guilt.

He tossed down the glass of whiskey and poured another.

~ * ~

Landis pulled the slim cellular phone from the side pocket of her suitcase and found the scrap of paper with Paula's home phone number on it. She took both and locked herself in her small bathroom.

It was ridiculous to be so nervous. No one could hear her, yet her hand shook as she dialed the number. After several rings, a machine picked up.

"Leave a message," the answering machine instructed.

"The least you can do is answer the phone," Landis fumed. "I've met your victim, and—"

"Landis?" came Paula's slightly flustered voice.

"No, it's the Tooth Fairy," Landis snapped.

"Are you in the house?"

"Yes."

"Paula, what is it?" Landis heard a sleepy male voice on the other end of the line.

"Just a minute," Paula said quickly.

37

Landis knew who that voice belonged to.

"All right," Paula said breathlessly. "Did you have any trouble with your cover story?"

"No. Roll over and tell Bill Gaiser the fake resume did the job."

Paula ignored the comment. "Did you learn anything? Any family or housemates that will do us any good?"

"First, let's get this straight," Landis said. "There is no 'us.' I'm being forced into this James Bond crap. And, no, there isn't anything here that would be of any interest to you and your fans."

"Damn. No live-ins or loony relatives?" Paula prompted.

Landis thought of Orphy Salankewietz. She wouldn't call the woman loony...exactly. Just colorful. "No one," she snapped.

Paula cursed. "Maybe Cain's gay. Are there any pretty young men in the house?"

"You're sick. You know he's straight."

"Well, I may be sick, but I'm also the woman who holds your career in her hands. Bring me back a story. Got it?"

"Sure," Landis said, almost strangling on the words. "I will bring you back the truth. And if you try to twist my words into something else, I'll—"

"You'll what?" Paula snarled.

"I'll go to the Pittsburgh Broadcasters Association and expose you." She snapped the phone shut and, storming out the bathroom door, threw it into her suitcase.

Landis knew she posed no threat to Paula. The PBA wouldn't care if Paula used a ouija board to get a story.

No matter what she did she couldn't stop this train wreck from happening. If she refused to turn in a story Paula would have her fired, and some other poor slob would have to get the story. If she said the Cain household was a perfect home, she would still be guilty of invading his privacy.

She couldn't win.

She took a hot bath, then dressed in her nightgown and crawled into the strange bed, pulling the covers up under her chin. She knew she would be a long time getting to sleep.

~ * ~

In the small room tucked beneath the eaves of the house, Edward Richards listened carefully as the house grew still. With the adaptations he had made to the intercom system he could hear anything that happened in the house: the click of stemware in the dining room, the harsh repetition of the old woman's snores—and the soft, feminine sound of Landis Delaney slipping into her new bed.

For a brief moment he regretted not putting an intercom in the bathrooms, especially when he heard her muffled voice through the bedroom wall. She must be one of those people who sing in the shower. He would have liked to listen to her. But that didn't really matter. He heard everything he needed to hear, saw everything he needed to see, and he knew that Ramsey's personal assistant was going to be trouble. He could feel it in his bones.

She had a certain appeal, he supposed—young, fresh, with an air of innocence about her.

Innocent, like his beloved Holly. The words burned into his brain.

Not that she looked like Holly. Not at all. This one was pale and freckled. Holly had been dark and exotic, with hair the color of chestnuts and eyes of deep emerald green. Holly had held herself with elegance, even as a child. This one was lithe but lacked Holly's regal charm.

She was a pitiful substitute.

Oh, he had seen the way Cain looked at her and knew what those heated glances meant. Cain had begun to come out of his mourning, feeling the pull of the world again. But it was a world the man had no right to. Not when Holly lay in her grave. A grave to which Ramsey Cain had condemned her.

This *assistant* was a distraction Edward would allow...for now. It would keep Cain occupied, give him hope, make it all the more painful when that hope was crushed. Just as Holly's hopes and dreams had been crushed.

It was time to tighten the noose around Ramsey Cain's neck.

His own plan was poetic. Reaching out, he stroked the long gray braid of the wig on the stand next to the mirror. As the trusted housekeeper he could go anywhere, see anything, and no one would suspect, until he was ready to strike. He would continue to remind Cain of his guilt, then, when the time was right he would pounce. He would make Cain suffer the tortures of the damned, and the little redhead would be his unwitting accomplice. He would make the man pay for what he had done.

And then he would send him to Hell.

Four

By midnight Ramsey was too tired and too drunk to wait any longer. He drew himself up from the chair, and knocked the empty whiskey decanter to the floor. On less-than-steady legs he climbed the stairs, and glanced over his shoulder at the tiled foyer floor.

Holly still tormented him. Even when she failed to make her usual visit the wait was torture.

Ramsey had almost convinced himself this night would be a calm one, that his late wife would stay in her ethereal realm. But as he crossed the landing at the top of the stairs a familiar chill swept over him.

He turned to the railing, gripping the century-old oak for support. Below on the tile floor the mist had begun to gather. Perhaps it was the whiskey. He strained against his fatigue and the liquor to focus his eyes and greet his ghostly wife.

~ * ~

Landis was in a place between dreams and the last fragments of the day when something invaded her peace. Instantly wide awake, she listened, senses keenly alert.

For the span of a heartbeat, she sat very still; then, as quickly as her nerves would allow, she bolted from the warm bed. Slipping on her robe and slippers, she unlocked the door and swung it open.

The hallway was dark, and she had begun to close the door again when she saw Ramsey in the dim light at the top of the stairs. She moved silently into the shadows of the dark hall to watch him.

His attention was on the foyer, and his lips moved as though he spoke to someone below. She inched forward, secure in the knowledge that the shadows hid her from view. She wanted to see to whom he spoke in such low and menacing tones.

Tension held his entire body rigid. He gripped the rail so tightly his knuckles showed white against the tan of his hands. His face was a mask of deep concentration and...fury.

She knew instinctively she'd intruded into his private world, and caution made her back away. She'd forgotten the small table and glass hurricane lamp behind her, and she stopped barely short of toppling both to the floor. She caught the lamp and righted the table, but not quietly enough.

"Who's there?" Ramsey called.

For a moment she toyed with the idea of making a mad dash for her room, but his gruff tone as he repeated the demand told her it was no use. Better to face the music than start her new job under a cloud of suspicion.

"It's me, sir," she said in a mild, timid voice.

"Landis?" Ramsey stepped toward her into the shadows. "What are you doing?"

What was *she* doing? He was the one lurking in the dark hallway. Well, all right, technically she had been lurking in the dark hallway as well, but only because he was talking to...who *had* he been talking to?

"I heard someone out here." That wasn't a lie.

"It was only me," he said, softening his voice.

Funny, Landis thought, how distracting the effect of that voice could be.

"I guess my aunt was right; my prowling does rattle the house."

He moved even closer, and Landis looked up into his face. The tension was still there, in the corners of his eyes, the creases on his high forehead. The dark beauty of that face awed her, but the faint scent of whiskey surprised her.

Was he drunk?

"I'm sorry if I disturbed you," she said.

"I was already disturbed," he answered. That soft rumble in his voice and the way he studied her features started a trembling in her stomach that coursed up her chest and into her arms.

She needed to move away from him, needed distance to think clearly. She managed to get past him and stopped by the railing at the top of the stairs in the pale light. A quick glance toward the stairs revealed nothing there but a cold draft that seemed out of place on this warm summer night. "Well, as I said, I heard a noise."

"And you bravely came to investigate. What did you expect to find?"

"Nothing...I don't know. I wasn't snooping," she said a bit too defensively.

"I should hope not."

He turned and moved toward her again, destroying her momentary sense of control.

Did he suspect she *had* been snooping? Landis tried to read his eyes, then nervously turned her attention to the foyer again.

"There isn't anything there," he said flatly.

"What?" She was so off-balance now she wasn't sure what she thought anymore. God, she hated feeling this out of control, especially when *he* was so obviously in perfect control...despite the whiskey.

"Whatever you were looking for isn't there, either in the foyer or in my eyes." Ramsey reached out and touched the confusion of curls at her temple.

She needed to get a little control of this situation; and, more importantly, she needed to compose herself. "Who were you talking to?" she asked. His eyes narrowed, his face tensed, and his hand dropped to his side. He obviously hadn't expected that question.

Good For a moment she had the upper hand.

"Your voice rattles the house even more than your feet," she said, pressing the advantage.

"You heard me? I thought what you heard was a noise."

"I heard your voice. I didn't hear what you were saying." Landis's advantage had begun to slip away.

"But you *weren't* snooping?" He raised a brow.

"I was curious why you were up so late." She knew she was pushing it but couldn't seem to help herself.

"I keep late hours."

"But who..." That made no sense. He had been talking to someone...hadn't he?

"There was no one else here." Again he seemed to read her thoughts. The comment was delivered with a calm that sent a chill down Landis's spine. "There is so much you do not understand, so many things that I can't explain."

He seemed perfectly rational and Landis began to wonder if she weren't the one with the problem.

"Perhaps," he said, "we could discuss this tomorrow?"

"But—"

"Good night, Landis." he said firmly.

The wall around him closed once again, firmly in place, and Landis knew the discussion was over. She turned and, trying not to seem in a hurry, escaped to her room.

~ * ~

Ramsey watched her go with ambivalence. He didn't want to answer her questions. Looking into those clear, pale eyes and lying was more than his frayed emotions could stand. But he didn't want her to leave, either. He wanted to draw her curves into his arms and smell the lingering scent of sunshine in her hair.

God, what a disaster this was.

On the one hand he had his wife, who had been cold and tormented even before death had claimed her. On the other, he had Landis. Or he wished he had Landis!

She was warm and soft, and, oh, so sexy. She had put on a silky white robe but had forgotten to tie it shut, giving him an eyeful of creamy leg from the hem of her satin pajama shorts to the beady-eyed teddy bear slippers on her feet. It was almost distraction enough to make him forget she'd been spying on him.

He had seen her in the shadows even before she'd nearly toppled the oil lamp, and startling her had seemed the only way to bring her out of hiding. By that time Holly had returned to the ether, but he hadn't relished the idea of Landis seeing any part of his guilty scene.

And exactly when had he so lost control of his desires? His painful reaction to her sexy little pajamas was as much a surprise to him as finding her watching him from the shadows had been.

He stifled a laugh as he traced her footsteps down the hall and, resisting the urge to stop at her door, went through the office and into his own room.

For the first time in a very long while he felt alive. The blood hammered in his veins. Hell, he might even need a cold shower.

~ * ~

Some time later, Ramsey stepped out of that cold shower and, wrapping a thick towel around his waist, padded silently across his bedroom. The tiny clock on his nightstand claimed it was nearly four a.m. He was tired, but not tired enough to sleep.

He had worked out on the machine that dominated the corner of his room until the sweat ran off his body in streams. Then he stood under the cool shower until his skin began to shrivel. Finally, his desire receded to a dull ache in his temples, but desire hadn't been his only problem.

Oh, there had been guilt. There was always quilt, but tonight there seemed to be an even more dangerous demon. Hope. Such a harmless-sounding word, but one that could spell disaster to someone who knew it was only an illusion. It had been so long since he had even glimpsed it, God knew, that a sudden influx of the real thing would likely poison him.

But that was what Landis Delaney represented: hope and dreams and honest blue eyes and teddy bear slippers. He wanted more. Like a drunkard returned to the bottle after years of sobriety, he wanted to drown in her presence. He wanted to rub that warmth and light into his skin, feel it seep into his cold bones and his icy heart.

He dressed in his black silk pajama bottoms and matching robe and slipped quietly into the office. Just to be closer to her, he told himself. But when he put his hand on the doorknob that led to her room and it turned, he was no longer sure where this need would take him.

For a while he stood at the foot of her bed. A shaft of pale moonlight angled low in her window, flooding her bed with blue-white light. She had twisted in the sheets, her legs curved elegantly on top of the covers while her shoulders snuggled beneath. The moonlight kissed her soft mouth and made her skin look like fine porcelain.

She took his breath away.

Landis turned suddenly, and Ramsey waited, truly holding his breath. If she awoke and found him there she would no doubt scream the roof down, and rightly so. He was mad. It was madness that drew him into the bedroom of a stranger. And madness that made him grieve for the fact that she was a stranger, and that she would have to remain one, for her own good.

He found the robe she had worn earlier draped over the foot of the bed. He gathered the satin in his hands and pressed it to his face. The whispered caress of the fabric, the faint scent of her perfume, invoked a thousand fantasies. It promised him the touch of her soft skin, the scent of her hair, her warm body...

As silently as he had come, he dropped the robe onto a chair and left her room. He crossed the office to his own room and closed the door behind him.

Tomorrow he would explain to her that he suffered from insomnia, that sometimes he even walked in his sleep, and he would suggest that she consider locking her door.

~ * ~

Landis shut off the ringing alarm clock and groaned. Six-fifteen. She hadn't gotten to sleep until well after two, and then she had spent the rest of the night caught in the grip of a restless dream.

In her dream she couldn't feel the carpet beneath her bare feet, but she could see her toes peeking from beneath her robe with each step she took. When she looked up, she found herself standing at the door to Ramsey's office. The room was dark except for the noiseless flash of lightning beyond the tall windows. A sudden brilliant flash cast its stark illumination on a figure standing at the window.

Fear rose up inside her, stifling a cry that froze in her throat. He turned, his face lit by a force she could not identify, and called to her.

"Landis."

Her name was a plea, an overture that slipped from his lips and pulled her to him. Without thinking, she went into his outstretched arms.

His mouth captured hers, parted her lips, and began an artful quest, deeper and deeper, until she couldn't breathe, couldn't think beyond the kiss, the hands that touched her skin, the body that pressed hot and needful against hers. She could almost feel him slip into her, through every pore in her flesh. She felt him in her head, her breast, her aching body.

The floor beneath her feet began to buckle, but she thought nothing of it. He was there. He would hold her safe and secure. But he didn't. He faded, vanished, as had the floor, leaving her panicked and empty and miserably, miserably cold.

She began to fall. She tumbled over and over, down a seemingly endless flight of stairs. When she stopped, she floated above herself. She saw herself lying below, her pale body crumpled on the marble tiles of the foyer floor, her lifeless eyes staring up at the man at the top of the stairway. The man who had loved her and had let her die.

Shaking her head to clear it, Landis sat up in bed and muttered a curse. It was this spooky old house, she told herself, stumbling to the bathroom. She needed a hot shower and her normal morning routine to forget her midnight confrontation with Ramsey and the dream's unsettling images.

But the nagging feeling that the dream had been important stayed with her as she showered, shampooed her hair, and rubbed the thick terry-cloth towel over her body. When she looked at herself in the foggy mirror she saw the same face she had the day before, but her eyes revealed something different in them.

It's this place, she told herself again, her new boss, and the gothic atmosphere that surrounded her. Nothing more.

She wrapped herself in the towel and went to the closet to find something to wear, something business-like and suitably prim and drab. As she left the bathroom she noticed her robe on the chair.

She hadn't left it there. She always threw it on the foot of her bed in case she needed it. She had been doing so since she was a child. She picked it up and, eyeing the foot of the bed, tossed it there.

She had long been a creature of habit. Her clothes were hung in her closet a certain way, her dresser drawers were always arranged with the same articles of clothing in the same drawer, and her dressing table always had a certain rhythm to it. It had been the one constant when she moved from her parents' house to the college dorm and from there into her own apartment.

Maybe she was losing it. With all this spy-versus-spy stuff it would be no wonder. But the robe nagged at her as she chose an outfit.

Dressing quickly in a dark skirt and plain cream-colored blouse, she sat down at the dressing table and plugged her blow dryer into the outlet.

By the time she walked down the hallway she felt more like herself. That was, until she stepped into the empty dining room. She glanced at her watch; it was exactly seven o'clock. Ramsey had told her breakfast was at seven, and she had expected to find him and his aunt sitting at the big, mahogany table. She wandered through the swinging door into a cozy kitchen.

Catching sight of Landis, a plump woman in a rumpled apron gave her a broad smile. "Well, you must be the new secretary. I wondered if you'd make it in to visit me?"

With her rosy cheeks and quick smile she reminded Landis of all the fairy godmothers who always turned up in fairy tales.

"Queenie told me to fix you something light, but I bet you're an eater," the cook said.

"Queenie?"

"Her highness, Lady Eberhart, royal pain in the arse." She dusted her flour-covered hands on her apron and extended one to Landis. "I'm Ivy McCreary."

"Landis Delaney. It's a pleasure to meet you," Landis clasped her hand and returned the woman's warm smile.

"Pleasure to meet someone *normal*, you mean," the cook said and giggled at her own joke.

"Does Eberhart get to decide what we eat?" Landis asked, following Ivy to her stove.

"More's the pity." Ivy took down a cup, filled it with aromatic coffee, and handed it to Landis. "She's the housekeeper, in the old meaning. She runs the house. After the missus died I had my hands full with the kitchen, and the rest of the staff left."

"Doesn't Mr. Cain handle the household affairs?"

Ivy gave a derisive snort and shook her head. "You want pancakes or oatmeal?"

"Pancakes. Thank you."

The cook clasped her hand to her heart. "Hallelujah. I *thought* you were an eater. I was worried, with that tiny waist, you'd be the picky, rice-cake sort of girl."

Landis sat at the battered old table and smiled at the stack of pancakes the cook placed in front of her. "Food is my weakness."

She doused the cakes with thick maple syrup and was about to dig in when she remembered the empty dining room. "Where is everyone? I thought Mr. Cain and Mrs. Salankewietz ate breakfast at seven?"

"I start to serve breakfast at seven," Ivy said, washing out the oatmeal pot. "Queenie eats a little earlier. No one takes the morning meal together. Orphy eats there..." she pointed to the table. "Alone. Then she heads off to the Wal-Mart or the McDonalds or one of the other places where those with time on their hands can go to play bingo. And himself—Mr. Cain—takes coffee in his rooms, but never before noon. It ain't natural, but you'll find a lot in this house that ain't natural."

The door from the dining room swung open, and Eberhart swept in. Landis noticed she moved as though she were the lady of the house instead of the housekeeper.

"Good morning, Miss Delaney," she said curtly.

"Good morning, Eberhart."

"I've a bone to pick with you," Ivy McCreary said, turning on the housekeeper. "If you want to continue to eat, you have to tell Mr. Cain I need more money for food."

"You're given more than enough funds," Eberhart snapped.

"You're telling the wrong person," Landis said to Ivy, though she wasn't sure why she wanted in this argument.

"I beg your pardon?" Eberhart turned a stern eye on her.

"Taking care of the house is your business, but taking care of the kitchen is Ivy's. If she needs more money from Mr. Cain she should tell *him*, not the housekeeper," Landis said, wiping syrup from her mouth.

Eberhart straightened her spine and closed her eyes as if to dismiss Landis's opinion entirely. "I have been put in a position of authority over the entire house, and I take those duties very seriously."

"I see that you do," Landis said, making an effort not to sound sarcastic. But it appeared that even agreeing with Eberhart made her angrier because the housekeeper's expression only darkened.

"I would thank you to keep to your own duties. Whatever *they* might be." The last was said with a snide tone and a critical arching of one eyebrow.

Landis raised an eyebrow of her own. "What does that mean?"

"Everyone here knows you were hired to see to the needs of the *man*, not his house." That said, the housekeeper sailed through the doors into the dining room.

Landis glanced back at Ivy, whose apple cheeks had deepened several shades.

"What did she mean?" Landis asked.

"Well...Mr. Cain's been alone so long...and suddenly he needs an assistant." The cook nervously strangled the dishtowel in her hands. "And you're such a pretty thing..."

They thought she had been brought there to..."That's crazy. Mr. Cain had no idea what I looked like." Landis laughed nervously.

The thought was too ludicrous but it sent an unexpected tingle through her nervous system. Ramsey

Cain had hired a secretary, though he had never bargained on one who supplied information to someone such as Paula Rice. But to think that a secretary would do more than office work was...antiquated.

"Thank you for breakfast, Ivy, and for the laugh. I needed it this morning." Landis left the baffled-looking cook and started for the office.

She paused at the foot of the steps. She wondered if she would ever pass by there without feeling uneasy. She pushed those thoughts away, hurried up the stairs and down the hall toward the office.

She had let Ivy think Eberhart's comments meant nothing, but with each step that took her closer to the office her anger grew.

See to the needs of the man—as though she were some medieval chambermaid sent to polish his lordship's boots...or his armor...or what ever he wanted polished. By the time she reached for the door she was close to a full-boil temper.

~ * ~

Ramsey glanced up as she came through the door and his heart slammed into his ribs. Her hair was a cloud of fire haloing her face. Funny, he hadn't noticed the bright morning light streaming through the tall windows before that moment. It was as if her presence in the room lifted invisible blinds, flooding the room with dazzling warmth and life.

"Good morning," he managed around the dull ache that blossomed in the pit of his stomach.

"Good morning." Her reply was distracted, cold and decidedly non-Landis-like. Her gaze skipped around the room, then settled on him. Ramsey got the impression she wanted to say something and wasn't sure where to start.

"Is something wrong?" he asked.

She laughed, but even to a man unused to hearing laughter it sounded hollow.

"Wrong? What could be wrong?" she snapped, then paused a moment to give him that direct look that so enchanted him. "The housekeeper insinuated that sleeping with you is part of my job description. Other than that everything's just hunky-dory."

~ * ~

Landis planted her hands on her hips, challenging him to deny it. His gaze on her face was as tangible as a breeze caressing her flushed cheek.

He came out of his chair and circled the desk. He stood too close again, intimidating her without even trying; but she managed to stand her ground, which happened to be directly beneath his heated gaze. She looked up into his dark, exotic face. "She did?" he asked, furrowing his brow.

"Yes. What are you going to do about it?"

He smiled that brief, honest smile that melted her anger, then turned to face the tall windows. "What can I do? If Eberhart believes it, nothing I do or say will likely change her mind."

Landis followed him to the window, positioning herself so he couldn't turn his back on her again. She wasn't fooled for a moment. He was enjoying this. "Like hell it won't. It's the truth. She'll have to believe you."

"But we're not sleeping together. Why would I tell her we are?" he asked, a small smile turning up his mouth.

"No! You have to tell her we're not sleeping together—oh, you know what I mean!"

She waited for him to say something more, but instead he reached out and brushed a curl from her forehead. She should have slapped his hand away, but she stood very still, looking up into his hypnotic eyes, and wished his nearness and all this talk of sleeping with him hadn't had such an odd effect on her.

"Why would Eberhart think you were my lover in the first place?" he asked, and for a long moment Landis stared at him.

Stubborn and patient. He had her off-balance, and he knew just how to keep the advantage, just how to keep her off-balance.

He watched her again with that shadowed gaze, and when she didn't answer his question, he posed a new one. "Why would Eberhart have any insight into the reasons I needed a secretary?" he asked.

"I don't know—maybe you told her something."

He cocked an eyebrow, and that barest hint of a smile touched his lips. "Do I look like the sort of man who would confide in his housekeeper?"

"No," Landis admitted softly. He looked like a pirate, with his hair brushing soft on his shoulders and eyes that caressed her face. He filled her head with impossibly erotic notions. His features, even lit by the full light of the sun, seemed eclipsed by something darker than night, more fearsome than hints of murder. He was a pirate of souls.

He is only a man, her logical mind told her, flesh and bone; letting her ungovernable imagination build him into something more invited trouble.

"I admit you're a temptation to a poor, lonely widower," he said in a voice that rumbled up from deep in his chest.

Landis decided it was time to get away, but for some reason she could not make her legs obey. Her arms hung like lead at her sides, and her feet seemed bolted to the hardwood floor.

"Are you shocked?" he asked, his warm breath fanning her cheek.

"No," she said, too timidly. She could do little more than look up at him and will herself not to tremble. He was an energy she could feel in the very air she breathed into her lungs.

The finger that had brushed the hair from her face now traced the line of her cheek and jaw and tipped her face up to meet his fiery gaze.

"Are you afraid of me, Landis?" he asked, so quietly she could barely hear him over the thump of her heart. "Does the thought that I might find you attractive frighten you?" As he watched her, waiting for an answer she could not give him, his face changed. The stern set of his features grew thoughtful; his gaze moved over her face, then stopped to study her mouth.

The thought hit her so suddenly it sapped the last of her strength. He was going to kiss her.

She waited breathlessly as his head dipped and his mouth descended. The contact was a feather's touch before his arms pulled her closer. Landis couldn't think. She could only react, and her reactions were disastrous. She leaned into him, opened her mouth to his carnal possession, and lost all reason.

~ * ~

Ramsey felt the kiss in every cell of his being. The taste of her, the smell of her, the feel of her burned itself like a brand on his soul. He deepened the kiss, taking everything she so foolishly gave and demanded more. He crushed her impossibly soft body to his, wishing for one irrational moment that he could hold her forever.

If she had only resisted, pushed at him or fought, he could have chalked the whole incident up to his abominable nature, but she didn't. Her small, graceful hands on his shirt front gathered the fine linen into her firm grip. She brushed her tongue against his in an unpracticed, if not totally naive gesture that damn near made his knees buckle.

He kissed her, and kissed her more, until he realized exactly what he was doing. As gracefully as he could without throwing himself across the room, he released his hold on her wondrously soft mouth and held her away from him.

After an eternity, she blinked her wide, blue eyes and brought her fingers to her lips.

"Perhaps you *should* be afraid of me." It was a statement spoken just above a whisper.

"Do I have reason to be?"

Ramsey backed away as though she had burned him. And she might have done just that. His entire body felt feverish and, like the chills that come with a fever, cold as ice.

He turned to the window. For a long moment she stood beside him in the silent office while he willed himself to breathe, hoping to clear his head.

"I think, in the future, you should ignore Eberhart," he said, his voice perfectly controlled. "Now, if you'll excuse me, I have calls to make this morning."

It was a dismissal, and if Landis ran for the door he wondered if she would ever be able to face him again.

"I can place the calls if you like," she said, surprising him by the calmness of her voice.

"That won't be necessary. Take the morning to get familiar with the house. This afternoon you can start your work."

This time Landis took the chance he offered. She walked out of the office and into her room. Ramsey waited for her to leave before returning to the desk. She *was* afraid of him, and she had every right to be, he thought grimly.

Holly! Every road in his miserable life led back to her. Landis feared him because he could not control his passions and because she thought he had murdered his wife. It carried him back to that night, to the whiskey, and the vision of his wife lying at the foot of the stairs, her head haloed in a pool of blood.

There was no point in reliving those moments. He couldn't change any of it. He ran a hand through his hair, trying to force his mind to clear. He'd made another miserable mistake. He felt something for this woman and he had acted on it. He should send her away, for his own sake, if not for hers. God knows, any reasonable woman would have bolted for the door, pausing only to call a good lawyer. Not Landis. Despite her fear of him, she hadn't run when he kissed her. Hell, she had kissed him back with enough passion to kick his libido into overdrive.

Some part of him wanted to believe Landis wouldn't want to go. Another part wanted to think that if his forgetfulness or confusion or whatever it was consuming his good judgment along with his mind got too bad he'd insist she leave. He would ignore his desires and dismiss Landis, fire the staff, and send Aunt Orphy on one of those senior citizen cruises.

If this madness got too bad, he would face his demons alone. That way, at the very least, they wouldn't have to watch him self-destruct.

Five

Landis opened the door of the office just after lunch and found Ramsey bent over his drafting table. He looked up and glared as though she were interrupting.

"I'm sorry," she said automatically, then could have bitten her tongue. She didn't have anything to be sorry for; she was supposed to be this man's assistant.

"I'm working," he growled.

She ignored his gruffness and his request for solitude. "I'm going to start on the files." He ran an impatient hand through his hair, exhaled sharply, but said nothing. She kept an eye on him as she crossed the room to the filing cabinet.

The man was a mystery!

Earlier he had melted her will with a kiss. He had tried to intimidate her and to make her feel...what? She wasn't sure, but she did feel something. Now, he treated her with all the charm of a Scrooge. So why did her pulse quicken when he glanced up at her?

Impatience filled his dark shadowed eyes. Her instinct told her to leave him alone, to go about her business. Her instinct also told her she wouldn't find anything in his files that would constitute a story for Paula.

That had to be her priority, she reminded herself, not Ramsey Cain's eyes or the way his broad shoulders slumped over his work. She had to put together some kind of report and get the hell out of this house before he took it into his head to kiss her again.

"I have some questions," she said.

He sighed again, dropped his pencil, and looked up at her, an unreadable expression on his face. "By all means, ask them."

"You mentioned that you had misplaced things in the past...made mistakes. Is there anything I should watch for?"

"If you mean, do I become a drooling idiot, no!" His expression darkened. "I said I had made a few mistakes and that they had interrupted business."

"You said you misplaced a date book and had forgotten meetings..."

"Apparently, *you* have a very good memory," he snapped.

"Exactly, and I can keep your appointment book current for you."

He studied her for a moment, and Landis wondered if he was trying to decide if he could trust her. "I eventually found the date book. It's in the desk drawer," he said. "I have very little to keep track of these days. My business partner, Bridget Dunham, handles all the appointments and business relations. But I guess handling my date book does fall under your job description."

Landis opened the top drawer of his desk and found a battered leather day-planner lying on top of the general clutter. She lifted it and held it up. He nodded, and Landis flipped it open to the month, just to get an idea of what, if any, appointments he had lined up.

"You can see why I was lost without it," he said, turning his attention back to the drafting table.

She fanned through it, but found nothing in the pages—no addresses, no notations, no appointments—even dated as far back as a year.

It was completely blank.

"This is the planner that was missing?" she asked, working to hide her confusion. "Not a replacement."

"Yes. I've had it for years. Each year I manage to replace the date sections, but the phone numbers and contacts I've had since college."

She said nothing but closed it and carried it to her desk. He had no idea the pages in the book were blank. Something was very wrong. She placed it in the top drawer of her own desk and headed for the filing cabinet.

"May I ask how the date book came to be lost?" she asked.

"How does anything become misplaced?"

"And it just reappeared?"

"Why are you so interested?" Suspicion filled his voice.

"Just curious."

"Curiosity killed the cat."

She turned to stare at him. Was that a threat? Was it his way of warning her off the subject? "I'm sorry, Mr. Cain," she said stiffly.

He got up from the drafting table. "I thought we decided you were to call me Ramsey?"

"Ramsey," she said, but his name made her uncomfortable. She wanted—no, needed—the professional distance of calling him "Mr. Cain." The problem was, she didn't feel distant anymore. The kiss, his dark charm...something drew her in, linking her to this mysterious man.

"I can't tell you why my memory is suddenly so bad," he continued thoughtfully. "I never had trouble before..."

"Before your wife's death?"

He expression darkened. "Before Holly's death I managed things very well, even with a demanding schedule. Never had a distraction that I couldn't overcome. But, yes, I guess her death changed me."

"Changed you? How?"

"Before, I never had to wonder what people thought of me. Now, unfortunately, I know what they think." He turned to the window. Landis now understood the gesture as one meant to distance him from whatever he happened to be feeling at the time.

She placed her hand on his broad shoulder and a ripple of tension coursed through him. "What do they think?"

He turned to her, his eyes dark. "The same thing you thought. Ramsey Cain murdered his wife and got away with it."

His words hit her with the force of a glancing blow and left her momentarily dumbfounded. As she recovered, she found herself wishing she could refute what he said, wishing she could comfort him, even on the most superficial level. Instead, she carefully took her hand from his shoulder and turned to the filing cabinet.

Ramsey felt the absence of her touch as sharply as a winter wind, though he told himself it was what he wanted. He had chosen his words carefully to put this distance between them. Now he wanted to take them back, to keep her near him, to keep her hand warm and gentle on his shoulder.

No, he told himself, better to keep her at a distance and to remember what could happen if he didn't.

~ * ~

That evening Ramsey sent his excuses to the dinner table with his aunt, and Landis found the meal less strained with his absence. Afterwards, she opened the door to the office. She'd expected to find him in his office, diligently bent over his drafting table. To her relief, Ramsey was nowhere in sight.

She told herself to relax, that only a reporter would sneak into a man's office. And, no matter what, she wasn't a reporter; for today, at least, she was an executive assistant and had every right to get to work.

She turned her focus to the mountain of files she had sorted through and stacked that afternoon. As she suspected, they contained nothing that would help Paula's crusade. She felt a certain satisfaction in that. She planned to alphabetize the files, but considering her present mood she wondered how much she would accomplish.

Ramsey's empty date book—and that he didn't know it was empty—worried her. Was it just one of those moments of forgetfulness he had warned her about? Was there another date book filled with old names and numbers, tucked away in one of his desk drawers, that had momentarily slipped his mind, or was his mental state even worse than he had warned her it was?

She crossed the room to his desk and slipped open the top drawer. It was filled with the usual assortment of office supplies—pens, pencils, staples, notebooks, all of which were blank. Nothing out of the ordinary.

She moved down to the drawer on the right side and found more of the same. The bottom drawer held a notebook filled with sketches of rivers and meadows, all of them good but none possessing that spark that caught life. They were the sketches of an architect, not an artist.

The left side of the desk held more interesting things: a box of stale crackers, unopened sweepstake letters informing Ramsey he may have already won a million dollars, and a single black sock. But still there was nothing even slightly incriminating about the desk, no cryptic messages scribbled in a woman's handwriting, no forgotten date books filled with names collected over a lifetime.

Scanning the room, she closed the desk drawer and crossed to the table. Her gaze fell on a stack of blueprints neatly stacked on the drafting table. They were the ones he had been working on that afternoon, and though she knew little about architecture she could see that the unfinished lines were all in place, and the table was, surprisingly enough, neatly organized.

Ramsey had spent a productive day. It made her wonder if she worried about him for nothing.

Landis cleared a wide swath on the floor. She would need to lay the files out to get an idea of how they were divided.

~ * ~

In two hours Landis had plowed through the majority of the files, returned them to the cabinet, and, with the help of pink adhesive notes, tagged the ones that needed updating. She had made sense of Ramsey's jumbled system. Files of permits had been divided by date, rather than by company names, and names of individuals he dealt with were listed rather than the company they represented. It was a system that would work for only one person in the world—Ramsey Cain.

Even if she didn't find anything incriminating she was at least making headway as a personal assistant, unlike that afternoon when she had been too distracted by his presence to organize her thoughts, much less the files.

Of course, the files held no reminders of Ramsey and his soul-scorching kiss. She had reasoned with herself that the kiss was just the result of their argument and the dark longing that had suddenly appeared in her employer's eyes. It would never happen again...it couldn't, if she were to continue her hateful task of snooping on him.

Landis had gathered the last of the files from the floor and had them neatly alphabetized and back in the file cabinet when the doors to Ramsey's bedroom opened, and he stepped into the office. Immediately, the room filled with his presence. It was as tangible as a touch and affected her just as deeply.

He was so incredibly handsome, his sable hair falling around his face, his intense gray gaze finding and holding hers just a heartbeat too long.

"Good evening," he said softly and took a seat at the drafting table.

"Can I get you anything?" Landis asked, thankful she could make her tongue work at all.

"No, it's late. You can call it a day." He leaned down to the intercom on his desk and punched a button. The voice that told Eberhart to bring up a pot of coffee was somehow sterner than the voice he used when addressing her.

"I see you finished those blueprints," she said. Maybe getting him to talk would help dispel the uncomfortable tension in the air. "Do you need them sent out?"

He ran a hand through his hair but didn't turn to face her. "I called the shipping service, and they'll pick them up later."

"Do you need a label made?"

This time he turned a dark glare her way. "I can manage a simple shipment." His tone was sharp enough to cut, and Landis turned back to the files, determined not to offer any more assistance.

"Landis," he said after a few moments and an inpatient sigh.

Even if it was petty and juvenile, Landis wanted to ignore him. Instead, she looked up, surprised that his face had lost its hardness.

"I realize you're only trying to help. I'm just not used to having someone do this sort of thing. I had no right to snap at you."

That was his idea of an apology. She lifted one shoulder. "You'll get used to me," she said, deciding that would be the extent of her acceptance.

Neither spoke again until Eberhart appeared at the door, a pot of coffee and a single cup on a silver tray.

"Good night," Landis said, reaching past the housekeeper for the door knob.

"Just one moment, Landis. There is something I think I should clear up. Eberhart." That hard edge had returned to his voice. "You're paid to run this house. You're not paid for your opinions, nor do you hold any position of authority over any other employee in my home. Miss Delaney is *my* assistant. Furthermore, I've never known you to gossip—I'd prefer it remain that way."

Eberhart said nothing in her own defense, but a muscle twitched in the older woman's cheek.

"That's all," Ramsey said, dismissing her.

Eberhart took her cue and exited the office without giving Landis so much as a backward glance. Landis didn't watch Ramsey, but she could feel him move across the room. He poured the coffee and carried the steaming mug to his desk.

"Why did you do that?" she asked stiffly.

He took his seat and turned, giving her his most penetrating gaze. "Beg your pardon?"

"I said, why did—"

"I heard what you said. What did you mean?"

"Couldn't you have talked to her in private?" she said, unable to completely hide her anger.

"She offended *you*. I saw to it that she'll never do it again."

"Is that the way you deal with people? By making them feel stupid?"

"I hardly think I made Eberhart feel stupid."

"No, her, you ticked off," Landis said, suddenly unable to look him in the eye. "I was the one who felt stupid."

"You?"

"Yes. I feel like a tattletale running to the boss."

When she heard him rise from his seat, she managed a glance his direction. He was shaking his head, but that devilish smile had formed on his lips, playing at the corners of his mouth in a provocative way.

"I can't figure you out, Landis. One moment you're terribly worried about what the housekeeper thinks of you, the next you're angry at me for 'ticking off' someone who obviously does not hold you in high enough esteem."

"High esteem is all well and good when you're the boss. It doesn't mean as much to us peons. I have to work in the same house with that woman, as an equal."

"You're not her equal," he insisted, stepping closer.

"You're right; she has seniority."

"This isn't a union shop."

He stood too close again, and her heart fluttered in her chest.

"I wish it were," she said softly. "I could file a grievance."

"I think you will hold your own well enough." He spoke very softly, sending tremors through every nerve in her body. "If you can manage to keep your considerable passions in check."

"My passions!" she shouted, giving in to the urge to look up into his eyes again.

"Like that passionate display this morning."

"Passionate display..." she faltered. "Who kissed whom?"

"I kissed you," he said, raising a brow, then lowering his voice. "And you kissed me back."

He did it again, twisting the facts to keep her off-balance.

"It wasn't really a kiss," she said, folding her arms over her chest in a defensive posture.

His disarming smile widened. "Granted, it's been a while, but I definitely think that was a kiss—and a rather good one, if I do say so myself."

"It was manipulation, pure and simple."

"My dear Landis. Nothing I do is ever simple...or pure."

"You're doing it now—manipulating," she insisted, moving quickly past him to pace the office floor.

~* ~

It was an act of frustration, and Ramsey would have liked nothing more than to scoop her up as she walked past, to let her work off some of that frustration in his arms.

"You distract me because you don't want to discuss *your* problems," she said, folding her arms over her chest again.

"My problem is that you distract me," he answered, hoping to goad her further.

She covered her face with her small graceful hands and groaned softly. "Your problem is you have bouts of memory loss, a deplorable amount of ego, and absolutely no people skills."

"From that kiss, I would say my people skills are fine."

Landis turned toward her bedroom door. "You're impossible," she said.

He caught her. Encouraged when she didn't pull away, he pulled her toward him but managed to resist the urge to wrap his arms around her. "Whether or not I have what it takes to be a good boss is not the question. The question is, can you work for me thinking I might be tempted to manipulate you again?"

~ * ~

I'm in over my head, Landis thought frantically as she stared up into his stormy eyes. It was all a bizarre game, and she was just the top hat being moved around the board. Only one thing stuck in her mind. He didn't need saving; he needed a sparring partner, and she wanted to be it. It had nothing to do with her job at WALH or Paula. She didn't want to leave this man alone with his games and his bad memory.

"It all boils down to one thing," she said softly. "Can I trust you?"

He flinched. His brows furrowed and those dark clouds filled his eyes. He leaned toward her slightly and whispered, "No."

Eberhart opened the door, apologizing softly, and muttered that the messenger service waited downstairs for a package.

Landis wondered how she and her employee must have looked. Toe-to-toe, eye-to-chin, as though they were in the midst of something far too intimate. She suddenly didn't care if the nosy housekeeper thought she had caught them in a heated lover's quarrel. All that mattered was what he had said—she couldn't trust him, and, God help her, for some stupid reason she wanted to.

Pulling her arm away from Ramsey, she said a hasty goodnight and slipped through the door that connected her room to the office. She waited until the sounds had quieted in the office next door before taking her things into the bathroom. After a hot shower, she took out the cell phone, but this time she dialed a number she knew by heart.

Melba picked up on the third ring. Landis heard Marcus and Darren, her best friend's sons, scrapping in the background.

"Will you two cut it out?" Melba shouted, and Landis found the familiarity of the scene vastly comforting.

"It is so good to hear your voice," she said with a sigh.

"Landis! Thank you, Jesus," Melba said with her usual melodrama. "Are you all right? What's it like up there? What's he like?"

"I'm fine, safe, but I'm not sure how sound I am. It's very, very quiet, and he is everything and nothing like I expected."

"Is he still gorgeous?" Melba asked, a sultry note in her voice. "Kind of a pale Denzel Washington?"

"To you any handsome white man is a pale Denzel Washington," Landis laughed. "He looks like he did in the pictures, except I don't think he's seen a barber since the inquest."

"Damn, girl, those eyes and long hair, too."

Yes, Landis thought, those eyes, but instead of giving the head-to-toe description Melba wanted, she forced her friend back to work.

"I need you to check out a few people for me, and whatever you do don't get caught with these names at the station," Landis said.

~ * ~

Exiting the bathroom, Landis cocked her head and listened. Odd sounds came through the wall between her room and the office. A faint clink, like metal striking metal. It kept up a steady pace that compelled her to open the office door and peek inside.

The room was empty, but as she crossed the office the sound picked up in intensity. She tried to remember where she had heard it before.

Clank...Clank...Clank... It definitely came from Ramsey's bedroom. She pressed her ear to his door. The sharp sound of metal persisted along with other, softer sounds...grunts?...heavy breathing?

The gym! That was the sound. Ramsey must have a weight bench or something in there. It would certainly explain his remarkable physical condition, despite the fact that the man never seemed to leave his house.

Suddenly, she could see him so clearly: stripped to the waist, a pair of dark sweats hanging low on his hips, his damp hair clinging to his neck and shoulders, tiny beads of sweat tracing lines over his perfectly sculptured—

Whoa! Enough of that, she chided herself and, as silently and as quickly as she could, slipped back into her room.

But the mental images would not be banished so easily, and she knew sleep was a long way off. Slipping on her robe and slippers, she headed for the kitchen. What she needed was a hot cup of tea and time to relax, away from the erotic sounds coming from the next room.

She made it as far as the top of the stairs when a voice from the shadows of the east wing sent a frisson of momentary panic through her.

"Psst. Psst."

"Who's there?" Landis asked, squinting into the darkness.

Orphy stepped out of the shadows. "Having trouble sleeping, my dear?"

"Just a little restless."

"Come into my room. I'll brew a pot of tea, and we'll have a nice talk."

A talk was not exactly what Landis wanted, but she followed the old woman. Orphy Salankewietz doubtless knew more about Ramsey than anyone. If nothing else she might give Landis ideas she could pass on to Paula.

"Were you spotted, my dear?" Orphy asked with a toothy grin.

Landis felt suddenly very foolish, as though she were sneaking from one dorm room to another. And she felt guilty that her mission was to ferret out the family secrets.

Orphy carried the glass carafe to an automatic drip tea maker. "It's a pleasure to have someone to visit with. My nephew's wife never drank." She giggled, then added, "Well, not tea and not with me."

The comment obviously tickled the old woman because she giggled as she measured the tea leaves into the filter and started the pot dripping. She opened a small refrigerator and pulled out a carton of creamer, arranged it with cups, spoons, and sugar on a silver tray, and motioned for Landis to carry it.

"Ramsey's done very nicely for me with these little rooms." She indicated the furnishings with a wave of her hand. "When my Maury died I had no one but Ramsey, and he let me bring some of my things with me when I moved in."

Landis placed the tray on the oak table graced with hand-tatted dollies that sat between two stylish wingback chairs.

"Do you do your own tatting?" Landis asked. She waited for her hostess to take one of the seats and offer her the other.

"Good gravy, no," Orphy said, inspecting one of the lacy circles. "I bought those over in Amish country with some of my bingo winnings. A friend has a little shop and a lot more talent than I do. Ramsey will tell you I can't sit still long enough to do crafts. He says I'm afraid the Grim Reaper will catch me."

"You and your nephew are very close?"

Landis hoped to swing the conversation around to Ramsey. Now she wondered if Ramsey wasn't the very reason she had been invited to the old woman's private sanctuary.

"Maury and I were never blessed with children of our own. When my sister and her husband had only Ramsey, we all doted on him." Orphy gave an exaggerated sigh. "Everyone is gone now but me, and I'm afraid I haven't done a very good job of watching out for him these last few years."

Landis didn't know how to reply, so she waited silently for Orphy to continue.

"First, there was that disastrous marriage, then Holly's death, and now he seems determined to close himself off from everyone, including me."

The tea maker made a hissing sound and puffed a last burst of steamy air. "Would you fetch the pot, my dear?" Orphy asked, with a world-weary smile.

"Of course," Landis said, standing. "But don't think you can fool me with a helpless act. I've seen you move. You could still cut a merry polka if a handsome man asked you."

The old woman's chainsaw-like laugh filled the room, then settled into a wide smile that seemed to fold her face in on itself. "I'm an old woman. People expect a certain amount of fragility."

"Well, I don't," Landis said. Orphy reminded Landis of the women in her own family, and she returned the old woman's smile. "I have two grandmothers, a handful of great-aunts and a great-grandmother people still call when they have trouble with their arthritis."

"Was she a doctor?"

"No, but she can cook all sorts of horrible-smelling things that seem to work better than medicine."

That braying laugh pulled at Landis as she carried the teapot back to her seat and filled the cups.

"I would like to meet this woman someday," Orphy said and sipped her tea. "I think a bigger family would have done Ramsey a world of good. He was always too isolated. We were happy when he brought Bridget home, but they only became friends and nothing came of it."

"Bridget Dunham?" Landis asked, setting her cup down.

"Yes. Have you met her yet? She's a lovely girl."

"He used to date his business partner?"

"Well, they were in college then. They didn't start the company until much later."

"It's odd enough to remain friends with someone after you stop dating, but to go into business is very unusual."

"My nephew is a very unusual man, my dear," Orphy said with another broad smile.

Landis reached for her cup again and took a sip, hoping Orphy would pick up her story where she left off. After a moment of thoughtful silence, Orphy did just that.

"Then Ramsey's parents died..."

"An accident?"

"No." She took a trembling breath, and Landis felt a flash of guilt at pushing the memory. "My sister died of breast cancer, and John—Ramsey's father—died six months later. His heart. The doctors said it was a myocardial infarction. That must be Latin for a broken heart."

She took another pause, and Landis drank her tea, too touched by the old woman's words to push her any farther.

She didn't need a push. Orphy heaved a great sigh and continued. "It wasn't long afterward that Ramsey brought home Holly Richards. What a disappointment."

Landis tried not to appear too interested, but this was exactly what she had hoped to hear.

"She wore too much make-up, and her hair was always just so," Orphy remembered. "She said she came from a good family, but we found out later that was a lie. Her father abandoned them; her mother looked for men in bars and died a drunkard. They were dirt poor, and while that can make some people determined to do well all it did for Holly was make her grasping."

"Ramsey must have loved her." Landis hoped the gentle prod would keep Orphy talking.

"I'm sure he had some genuine feelings for her, but more than that Ramsey wanted to do the right thing." Orphy's weathered face grew sad again. "Holly told him she was pregnant. After the wedding, she claimed it was a false alarm, but by then the deed was done." She stared into her coffee cup. "I think Ramsey knew he'd made a mistake, but his sense of honor wouldn't let him divorce her. They lived in Pittsburgh for a half-dozen years, Holly playing belle of the ball, hostessing cocktail parties, volunteering for fashionable charity committees."

"Wasn't Ramsey happy?" Landis asked.

"Ramsey was happy as long as Holly was happy, and Holly was happy as long as she got what she wanted."

"What did she want?" Landis had become thoroughly engrossed in the old woman's tale. Wild horses couldn't have pulled her from the room.

"Money. The power that comes from having money. Her museum-quality townhouse in Upper St. Clair. Friends who thought she had quality. But then something happened." Orphy drew in her breath with a whistle. "Ramsey insisted they move back here. Holly was furious, but Ramsey dug in his heels, for the first time since they were married. They moved here, and everything turned bad."

"Holly wasn't happy here?" Landis asked softly.

Orphy's brittle laughter startled her. "That's an understatement. Holly was miserable. I fell and broke my hip, and Ramsey moved me into these rooms, which made Holly angrier. Ramsey withdrew, spending more and more time in the city. When he was here, he spent all his time remodeling that office.

"Holly drank," Orphy said, her voice suddenly a cold monotone. "And she raved about being isolated, accusing Ramsey of trying to drive her insane, accusing me of spying on her. When my hip had healed enough, I moved to Georgia, hoping that without my presence Holly might relax, but I think it was too late. A few months later she was dead, and they thought Ramsey did it."

This was said as though she had told a secret, and a thread of renewed guilt crept through Landis.

"You might find this hard to believe, but he wasn't always like he is now. He wasn't always so moody and cold. I know he couldn't have killed her," Orphy said, dabbing at her eyes, and Landis's own filled with unshed tears.

She sipped her tea in silence and waited for Orphy to collect herself. After a moment, Ramsey's aunt sniffled and straightened her shoulders.

"That's the past," the old woman announced

Landis feigned a smile. Was it the past? She might be responsible for bringing that past crashing down around them all again.

Unless...she could find a way to stop Paula.

Six

Above the eaves of the old house, Edward Richards sat at a small desk in the dark. With trembling fingers and quivering with rage, he shut off the small receiver.

The old bitch was spreading her filthy lies!

His father had not abandoned them. He had gone to find work and had died a hero's death saving someone else's life. His mother had told him all about it.

And his mother had been a beauty. Men had naturally flocked to her. But she was too much of a lady to accept their disgusting advances.

For a moment the memories pulled at him. The sounds he had heard late at night coming from his mother's room battered at him. No, he told himself. She had been having nightmares about his father's death. He didn't let himself remember the music, the laughter, the strong scent of cigarette smoke wafting on the night breeze. He remembered the scores of male family members who had come to pay their respects to the Widow Richards. They were uncles who gave him candy and soda pop. But that was all he would let himself remember. The doubts, fears, and suspicions of a little boy were put aside as he let the memory of his sister wash over him.

Ah, his beautiful Holly. Bright and charming, she had been more than a little sister. She had been his perfect, shining example of all a female could be: lovely, untouchable, innocent.

The old woman below couldn't spread her lies behind his back. He heard their dirty gossip. All of it. He had carefully rewired the intercom system to transmit with a flip of a switch on the control board in front of him. So he knew what they said, knew the damned lies they told.

Orphy Salankewietz would pay for her sins against Holly. And Miss Delaney...Miss Hot-Stuff-Secretary would pay, too.

A cruel smile twisted his thin mouth, and he studied his reflection in the mirror above the desk. He liked that smile. It was the smile of a villain. He would have to remember that smile when he made his triumphant return to the stage.

~ * ~

The dream had come again, and again Landis found herself on the stairs...but something was different. The strong arms that had drawn her in, that had held her briefly, the erotic rasp of his hard body against hers was missing. She knew he was there. The warm, intense presence that could only be Ramsey Cain was everywhere.

She opened her eyes, and for a moment lay on the unfamiliar bed staring at the shifting light on the ceiling above her head. The dream fell away, but the feeling of his presence remained, as sharp and real as the soft quilt that covered her trembling body.

She sat up and glanced nervously around the room.

"Is someone there?" she whispered, pulling the cover more securely around her neck.

There was no answer, but she couldn't shake the idea that *he* had been there, standing over her bed.

"Ramsey?" she whispered.

Was there a sound? Did the door latch click softly?

Shifting on the mattress, she leaned over and snapped on the lamp on the bedside table. The feeble sixty watts of light pushed back the shadows but fell short of chasing them away entirely. Landis needed a moment to adjust. She scanned the room—and found nothing.

The bed made a soft protest as she crawled out and, forgetting her robe, crept to the door that connected her room to the office. Just as she had earlier, she pressed her ear to the door.

Nothing!

She hurried back to her bed.

It wasn't bad enough that she dreamed about Ramsey, now she fantasized that he lurked around her room while she slept.

What would she have done if she had opened her eyes and found him standing over the bed?

Would she have screamed?

Somehow, she didn't think she would have. She would have held her breath. She would have listened to the hammering of her heart and waited to see if he would pull the blankets away, if he would stretch that long, perfect body out on the bed next to her. She wanted those strong arms around her, and that carnal mouth on her skin...

Landis pulled the covers over her head and threw herself back on the soft pillow. Where did this stuff come from? This sudden, erotic imagination she had developed would only drive her nuts.

She had never been a hopeless romantic. She had never indulged in fantasies that didn't have the slightest chance of coming true. Unlike Melba, who planned daily what she would do when Denzel Washington came to Pittsburgh to sweep her off her feet, Landis didn't buy that knight-in-shining-armor stuff. And if she had no one with the sense God gave string beans would have imagined Ramsey Cain in the part of Prince Charming.

Would they?

She'd had such a clear picture of him before she got a close-up. Now the edges of the picture were fuzzy, the lines blurred, and she didn't know what she saw anymore. Was he the cold-hearted killer she had believed, or the not-so-innocent victim of a cruel fate?

She wanted to know, and she didn't. She wanted to find something harmless that would still satisfy Paula. She wanted to get away from this house, and Ramsey. And the sooner the better.

~ * ~

The next morning Landis threw open the office door, then banged her knee painfully on the edge of the desk but managed to catch the telephone on the fourth ring. An uninterested Ramsey glanced up at her.

"Ramsey Cain's office," she said breathlessly, throwing him a stern look.

After a noticeable pause, an amused female voice said, "Well, good morning. Is this the new assistant?"

"Yes," Landis said, desperately trying to catch her breath.

"Tell Ramsey his beleaguered partner is on the phone."

"Good morning, Ms. Dunham," Landis said.

"What does she want?" Ramsey asked, furrowing his brow.

"Please, call me Bridget," Ramsey's partner said on the other end of the line. "What's your name?"

"Landis Delaney." She turned to Ramsey and mouthed. "What?"

"What does she want?" he repeated in a whisper.

"Is he shaking his head and whispering that he's not in for me, or is he still keeping vampires' hours?"

"I just got into the office; I'm not sure what he's doing." Landis glared at her boss, who had the nerve to smile at her.

"Well, you tell him that I forwarded those plans to Ludwig, Prentis and Fisk..."

Landis gathered a pen and tablet to take notes as Ramsey came out of his chair and crossed the room to stand at her elbow.

"The accident attorneys?" Landis asked, noticing the irritating nervous edge in her voice.

"Yes. They have the primary office space in the Riverfront Renaissance Mall project. Old Man Ludwig has a problem with the mall layout. He's also decided that he's tired of dealing with me and wants to speak to the man of the house." Landis heard Bridget curse under her breath. "Anyway, if Ramsey doesn't speak to this throwback,

Ludwig might pull out of the project, and we *really* don't want that to happen."

Landis covered the receiver. "It's about the mall project. Here he is, Bridget."

Bridget's laughter trickled through the long-distance line. "I like you. You're just what Ramrod needs, a woman who won't take any of his crap."

"Ramrod?" Landis repeated.

Ramsey groaned and reached to take the phone, but suddenly Landis didn't want to give it up.

"Why do you call him 'Ramrod?'"

"Just a name he picked up here at the office. I should tell you he can be a real terror with secretaries."

Ramsey took the phone before Landis had the chance to ask what she meant by the word "terror." "What are you telling her?"

Landis took her seat, but continued to pay close attention to her boss's conversation. Ramsey glanced at her. A faint smile twisted his mouth, and Landis felt heat blossom in her chest.

"She's working out fine," he said, making no more effort to hide the fact he was talking about her than Landis had when she'd been talking about him. "She has a few strange ideas, but all-in-all..."

Landis's mouth dropped open. Strange ideas?

"What does she look like?" Ramsey repeated, then laughed outright, a rich hypnotic sound that caused the heat in her chest to spread to her limbs. "I don't know...remember that cousin of Tony's who worked for us about a week? The one who had the huge crush on me?... That's the one. She looks like her, but taller, and she

87

doesn't have thick glasses... Red... I don't know; it looks real. Now, what's Ludwig's problem this week?"

Landis listened to the rest of the brief conversation; thankful it had turned from her to the usual interoffice stuff. They reviewed Bridget's fax containing the latest meeting with the law firm, and Ramsey didn't seem as concerned as Bridget.

Landis found her thoughts turning to Ramsey's comical, if somewhat less-than-flattering, assessment of her. He certainly hadn't seemed to be the sort of man who joked around with his co-workers. Of course, he had only her, Ivy McCreary, his Aunt Orphy, and Eberhart to interact with. Perhaps when he was with his partner in the city he was a very different man. She wished she had the chance to see him surrounded with friends, laughing and joking.

Landis waited until he hung up the phone, but he said nothing as he stood next to her desk and watched her with amusement.

"How did you get a nickname like 'Ramrod?' And why did Miss Dunham say you were a terror with secretaries?"

"Bridget has a big mouth," Ramsey grumbled. He didn't move away. Instead, he sat on the corner of her desk. Uneasy tension spread through her when he was so near. He held the advantage as long as he stood close, and she suspected he knew it.

"'Terror' is a very strong word," Landis said softly.

"Too strong." His voice was equally soft, but it vibrated in the pit of her stomach.

"I have never found a secretary who suited me."

"Never?" Landis wasn't sure why she asked such a thing, but his nearness compelled her.

"That remains to be seen." Again that smile pulled at the corners of his mouth, mesmerizing her. "Doesn't it?"

"You and Bridget know each other very well."

"Well enough." Ramsey's gaze moved over her face like a gentle touch.

"She's very fond of you," Landis said, watching closely for some sort of reaction. "That's nice, considering your history together."

Ramsey smiled at that and shifted on the edge of the desk. "And what do you know about my history with Bridget?"

"I know that the two of you were once...involved."

"We dated briefly, another lifetime ago," he said, studying her face. "We stopped short of being...involved."

"Still, you have to admit it's unusual."

"I've been told I can be very unusual."

Landis stifled a laugh. "That's exactly what your aunt said."

"So, Orphy's been filling you in on my life story."

"We talked," she admitted reluctantly. "Your aunt thinks the world of you."

"Blind loyalty."

"There didn't seem to be anything wrong with her eyesight. She loves you. She believes in you, but I think she has a clear picture of the kind of man you are."

"What kind of man do you think I am?" His finger traced the line of her jaw.

Landis ignored the question. "Your aunt thinks you're a good man who makes lousy choices."

"Your conversation must have been very thorough."

Landis's breath came out in a rush as Ramsey rose from his seat on the desk and crossed to the coffee pot on the cabinet. He moved very well. Most men his height stumbled through life, plowing into everything in their path. But he was different...graceful...completely in control of his body.

Landis pondered that thought a moment. What would it be like to be with a man like that? Would he be tender, that grumbling voice whispering in her ear? Or would he be demanding and forceful? She had only that kiss to give her a clue, and it had been a heart-stopping combination of styles.

Ramsey looked at her from a distance now, but with the same measuring gaze from those fathomless eyes.

"Coffee?" he asked.

Landis nodded, watched him pour it into a cup and bring it to her. "I'm supposed to be *your* assistant, remember?" she said around a catch in her throat.

He paused a moment and stared at her. "It's just a cup of coffee."

Ramsey sipped his coffee and went back to work. Landis tried to do the same, but wicked little thoughts hopscotched through her mind, not the least of which was his rather daunting nickname.

"Ramrod," she said with a soft giggle.

The glare he sent her was tainted with an amusement she knew he tried to hide. He jabbed a finger in her direction. "You are *not* to call me that."

"Okay," she said, smiling.

"I'm serious."

"I know."

"How am I supposed to maintain my reputation if people hear that ridiculous nickname?"

"No one will hear it," she promised. "There's no one here but you and me."

"*I* don't want to hear it."

"I should think you'd want to be rid of your reputation anyway," Landis muttered to herself.

"I heard that."

He was behaving very strangely, she thought. He was positively positive. Watching him sip his coffee and study the new set of blueprints in front of him, she wondered what had brought on this good humor. He had always seemed to Landis to be a man uncomfortable in his own skin, but not today. Of course, she was joking, too, and...flirting. She narrowed her eyes and studied him. What was different about today?

She shook her head and turned to her computer. The man really was a mystery.

~ * ~

At noon, Ramsey glanced up from his plans. He had almost forgotten Landis was in the room. Well, not completely. Her scent, that tantalizing mixture of vanilla and musk, had teased his senses, keeping her in the back of his mind. But he was comfortable, maybe even...happy.

Well, imagine that, he thought. Ramsey Cain, the man who needed no one, wanted no one to get too close; the man who hadn't been comfortable with any of the squadron of secretaries who had passed through his office in Pittsburgh, companionably shared his cramped office space with this strange, charming woman. And she made him happy without even saying a word.

That was probably it, he told himself. She made no demands, didn't seem to expect him to behave a certain way, or to be warm and fuzzy.

Hell! He had been harsh...cold...and except for those brief moments when she'd slipped past his defenses, downright mean. And still she had come back for more, quietly sorting messages and cheerfully clicking away at her computer.

Her computer. Her desk. Her chair. When had he started to think of them as hers? "I bet Mrs. McCreary has lunch ready," she said suddenly. He looked at his watch and rubbed the back of his neck. He was hungry, and it would feel good to get up and move around. He didn't usually eat lunch, but, then, he wasn't usually awake before noon.

"If you don't want to stop, I can bring you up a sandwich or something," she offered.

"No." He surprised himself by saying. "I could use a break."

He followed her out the door and down the stairs to the kitchen, but the look on the faces of the housekeeper and the cook when he stepped through the door made him wonder if he shouldn't have stayed in his office. The look of discomfort that passed between Ivy and Eberhart made him feel like an outsider in his own house and ended his unusually good mood.

Landis looked into Ramsey's stony face and saw the immediate change in him. Gone was the light-hearted Ramsey Cain. The other one had taken his place.

"What's on the menu, Ivy?" she asked, hoping to end the startled silence.

"A tuna salad and fresh melon," the cook said, coming out of her stunned stupor and hurriedly setting two places at the table. "If that's all right, sir?"

"Fine," Ramsey said brusquely.

Landis was sorry to see the sudden change in him. His staff would only see this Ramsey; the distant and cold man who joked with no one.

Eberhart, who had been seated on one of the battered kitchen chairs, stood rigidly and took a seat in the corner of the kitchen. Ramsey held the chair for Landis then sat at the far side of the table in the place vacated by Eberhart.

"I wasn't expectin' you, sir," Ivy McCreary said as she served.

"Should I have warned you that I was taking lunch in my own kitchen?" Ramsey asked, giving the woman a withering glare.

"No, indeed, sir," she said quickly and scurried away.

Landis glanced up from her plate after sampling the tuna salad. "This is wonderful, Ivy. My mother made tuna salad with macaroni just like this, and it isn't often made this way."

"Thank you, Miss Landis," Ivy said.

Landis waited for Ramsey to add his praises but he said nothing, so she nudged him with her foot. The look he gave her was one of pure shock.

"It's good salad, isn't it?" Landis asked him pointedly, nodding to Ivy who stood a few feet away, twisting her dish rag.

Ramsey, clearly flustered, muttered, "It's...fine."

"Thank you, sir." Ivy beamed, and hurried to the sink.

"Don't kick me," Ramsey whispered, leaning forward.

"I didn't kick you. I nudged you," Landis whispered in kind.

"Nudged, hell, that hurt," he hissed.

"It's customary to show gratitude when someone does you a kindness," Landis told him.

"She's my cook." Ramsey struggled to keep his voice low. "Doing her job isn't a kindness."

"That's true," Landis whispered back. "But she doesn't have to do it so well. For that, you should be grateful."

"Gratitude," Ramsey huffed. "I should be grateful that I was allowed in my own kitchen.

Landis sympathized, but, still, she knew she was right. "You're acting like some medieval lord of the manor. No wonder they treat you like a relic. No one is saying you don't have a right to eat in the kitchen, but when you suddenly change a lifetime of routine it causes a stir. Even medieval lords were followed out of respect, not fear. At least the good ones."

"Fear!" Ramsey shouted, then lowered his voice. "My staff doesn't know what fear is."

Landis set her fork aside and smiled. "Then you're a better boss than you think."

"Really? I thought I was too manipulative?" He narrowed his eyes. "Perhaps I should try *manipulating* Eberhart and Mrs. McCreary the way you seem to think I manipulate you."

He referred to the kiss, and her insistence that he had only done it to manipulate her. She glanced at Eberhart, who eyed them with suspicion. Landis stifled a laugh and looked back at Ramsey. Landis had a hard time imagining Eberhart kissing anyone. The thought was inconceivable.

"I don't think it would work on that one," she whispered, then noticed the cook watching her boss with a cautious expression.

"Is something wrong, Ivy?" Landis asked.

"I'd like a word with you, sir," Ivy said, obviously mustering her courage.

Ramsey reluctantly turned his attention to Mrs. McCreary. "What can I do for you?"

Landis knew he was trying hard to be the gracious employer, and knew, too, how difficult it was for him to put aside the medieval lord.

"It's about the kitchen budget. Well, sir, I need a bit of a raise. Prices being what they are, I'm having the devil's own time making the purchases I have to for you and Miss Orphy, and now with another mouth to feed..."

Ramsey looked uneasy. He turned away from the cook and cleared his throat as though he were suddenly unsure what to say to her. A smile flicker over Eberhart's face. That was odd, Landis thought, watching the housekeeper watch Ramsey. She could have sworn, when Ivy approached her with this request earlier, that Eberhart hadn't wanted Ivy to talk to Ramsey. Now, Landis wondered if the housekeeper hadn't expected just that reaction from her employer.

"The household accounts are handled by the company accountant in Pittsburgh, but I'll speak to him as soon as I can," Ramsey said. Rising from the chair, he stalked out of the kitchen.

"Did I do something wrong?" Ivy asked softly.

"No. Don't worry about it. I'll talk to him, and we'll get the money you need." Landis patted the woman's hand. "I hope."

As she followed Ramsey from the kitchen, she saw Eberhart's grin fade and an angry flash cross the woman's face. Landis made a mental note to find out what was up with that woman.

She heard Ramsey's voice before she opened the door to the office. He wasn't shouting, but the timbre of his voice was such that she could tell he was angry.

"...by tomorrow, Tony," he snapped into the phone. "I know the balance is low, but can't you move funds around? ... Well, out of the business reserves then... For God's sake, you can surely scratch up enough money for my cook to buy food? What about the last of the stocks, what was the price today?... If it holds there 'till morning, unload the last of it... I know what it will do to my portfolio, and I don't care. Just dump the last of my communications stocks. And remember, not a word to Bridget."

She knew she'd heard something she shouldn't have, but what? Was he telling his accountant to steal from his own company? She tried to decipher what was being said. He needed to free up money. Did that mean all his money was tied up? In the business? Was he having money problems?

Ramsey turned toward her and froze. Landis held her breath.

"I'll talk to you tomorrow, Tony," he said and ended the call with a brusque flick of his thumb. "How much did you hear?"

"I was just coming up to—"

"How much did you hear?"

Landis flinched at his tone. "More than you wanted me to."

"Would it have been too much trouble for you to let me know you were there?" he snapped. "Or were you snooping *again*?"

Ouch! Landis thought, a direct hit. "I wasn't snooping," she said a tad too defensively. "Now or ever!"

"But you did hear me?"

"That doesn't mean I know what you're doing or why. Unless you want to tell me."

The look he gave her said it all, a glower that warned her not to ask any questions. "Your duties have limits," he said calmly. "This is one of them."

He came toward her, with those graceful movements that made her chest tighten, and stood over her. He projected pure intimidation, she thought, looking up into his dark face.

"Don't listen to my private conversations," he said, his gaze holding hers a second too long.

"If you don't want to be heard, you should have private conversations in private," Landis suggested, a hint of sarcasm in her voice. "I am exactly where I have to be and—"

"You are treading on very thin ice here, Landis."

"All the ice around you is thin...sir." She was pushing it.

Ramsey made a frustrated sound deep in his throat and stepped away from her. Landis knew a split second of victory until those stormy, gray eyes met hers again.

"I have brought you into my home...into my life, and that gives you certain privileges. But don't think for one moment that it gives you the right to poke that pretty little nose of yours into every aspect of that life."

Landis opened her mouth in outrage, but it seemed a full minute before she could say a thing. "Privileges! What privileges? The privilege of being snarled at for trying to do my job, or the privilege of being kissed without warning...or provocation."

Ramsey narrowed his eyes. "Why are you so obsessed with that kiss?"

"I'm not obsessed!"

He gave her a coolly calculated look. "You certainly bring it up often enough."

"I—You—" Landis broke off with a frustrated growl. "You're impossible."

She slammed into her bedroom and stood so shaken with anger that it took her a while to realize he'd maneuvered the situation away from the conversation he'd had with this mysterious Tony person.

Fine, she thought. Let him think he had gotten away with something. It was just one more little secret she would know before she escaped Kinross House forever.

~ * ~

Ramsey resisted the urge to visit Landis's room that night, but struggling with his conscience left him restless. The weight bench helped expend only some of his energy;

the rest he tried to work off roaming the house after everyone else had gone to bed. That didn't help.

He was irritable, frustrated, and damn tired of being irritable and frustrated.

Landis Delaney, with her quick-tempered passions and fiery eyes, reminded him of everything he had deprived himself of for so long. The soft scent of a woman, the feel of satin and silk, the rasp of heavy breathing, that breathless moment before the body finds the release it so desperately needs.

He muttered a curse and closed the library door. His heavy footfalls on the stairs echoed forlornly through the house. Tonight, the only thing left was the whiskey bottle in his room and the hope that his dreams would be merciful.

The clammy chill that met him on the landing reminded him there was no mercy in this house. The mist had gathered in the foyer when his back was turned. Before he had time to brace his hands on the rail she began to materialize.

Ramsey watched and waited. The energy that had only a moment ago made him edgy drained away as Holly's diaphanous gown formed. It left him sick with emotion and shaken with rage.

Her face appeared in the mist. Cold and haughty, she stared at him, defying him to utter a word. Her lips did not move when she spoke, but he had found out the hard way that the dead had a way to speak directly to a man's heart.

"She's lovely, Ramsey."

It shocked him, though why it did was a mystery. Holly had always been able to find his weaknesses, and she had never failed to exploit them.

"She is of no concern to you," he said softly, conscious of how Landis had heard him the last time he had spoken to his dead wife.

"You can't replace me, darling," she drawled. "You're a fool to try."

In a heartbeat, the mist began to separate. Ramsey let loose the breath he had been holding. He stalked down the hall and into his office. Pausing for a fraction of a second to assure himself that Landis was asleep, he opened the unlocked door between her bedroom and the office.

His eyes, long used to the darkness, focused quickly, and he saw her lying on the bed. The covers were again twisted around her legs, and again her lashes lay softly on her pale cheeks. Throwing caution to the wind, he knelt beside the bed, his face mere inches from her.

"She's right," he whispered. "You are lovely." He wanted so much to touch her. Instead, he got to his feet.

Holly knew about Landis and his gentle feelings for her, but, then, Holly knew everything, didn't she? And now what? Would the vengeance Holly craved, even from the grave, spill over onto this innocent, beautiful young woman?

He drew a halting breath. "What have I done?"

Seven

Landis peeked into the office the next morning and found it empty. She wondered why she was relieved, and why the thought of facing Ramsey Cain always seemed so overwhelming? It had been daunting enough to keep her away from the dinner table the night before and, now, here she was hoping he wouldn't come in to work.

She told herself it was because of his anger the day before when he found her listening to his conversation. She told herself she wanted the time alone to do the one thing he had told her never, never to do—snoop. But deep down she knew the more time she spent in the company of the enigmatic Ramsey Cain the more she doubted herself and her chances of getting out of this situation emotionally intact.

She scanned his desk for any notes about the mysterious Tony, or why he'd had to bargain to get his own money. Then she lamented the fact that Ramsey was not the type of man who wrote down such things.

She had gone over the office very thoroughly the day before and knew if he kept any secrets in the house they were not here. So where did Ramsey keep his secrets? She glanced at his bedroom doors, then pushed that thought from her head. She would not—under any circumstances—sneak into his bedroom to look around...certainly not while he slept.

The library seemed the logical spot, and if that didn't work she could always figure out some way to identify this mysterious Tony. With any luck at all, she could find some way to get the information out of him.

She crept down the stairs as quietly as the old house would allow. At the foot of the stairs she took a huge step to avoid stepping on *that spot*. She knew it was childish but she'd begun to hate that place, and even the thought of stepping on it gave her chills.

Inside the very masculine library she took a moment to collect her thoughts. She hadn't had time to look around the elegant room the day she came to Kinross House. She'd been too engrossed in her new boss to notice the family pictures cluttering several shelves and the tops of every available surface.

There were several shots of a smiling couple taken over the years, one in front of a late-fifties model Thunderbird, another dressed in wedding clothes, still another smiling down at a baby. They reminded Landis of her own parents. They had that happy, contented look that so many couples are never lucky enough to find.

The most recent picture of the couple showed a handsome older man and a delicate woman smiling secretively at each other. Despite time, the bonds of love seemed even stronger than those in the earlier photos.

They had to be Ramsey's parents. He looked remarkably like his father, but had his mother's dark, intense eyes.

Other photos were of a dark-haired baby. "Ramsey Duncan Cain" was printed in gold lettering beneath one. The collection of photos showed him over the years, growing from a round-cheeked infant to an elegant young man.

Landis picked up what must have been a high school picture and gave an exasperated sigh. "God, he didn't even have the decency to be a gawky teenager."

She moved to a wedding photo in a beautiful silver frame. Holly Richards Cain beamed, her pure white dress clinging sensuously to willowy curves. But Ramsey did *not* seem as blissfully happy. His eyes held a haunted look, a look that had not been in any of his earlier pictures, a look Landis had seen for herself. Ramsey hadn't been happy on that day. His face told a story of a man who felt trapped.

Was that it? Had Ramsey been trapped in a loveless marriage? But why kill his wife? Why not simply divorce her—and why wait nearly a decade?

None of it made any sense.

"A lovely couple, don't you think?"

Landis jumped, knocking several of the photographs over, and Eberhart moved forward quickly to set them right.

"Don't sneak up on me like that," Landis said, pressing a trembling hand to her chest. She wasn't doing anything wrong, she reminded herself. At least she hadn't been caught rifling through the desk. How did so ungainly a woman develop such stealth, anyway?

"What are you doing in here?" the housekeeper asked in her usual frosty tone.

"Just looking around. Mr. Cain told me to take my time getting to know the place." Landis walked around the room. "I'm glad to see you. I was hoping you could answer some more questions."

Eberhart eyed her suspiciously, and Landis decided it would be best to dive right in. "What's up with the household accounts?"

"I don't know what you're referring to."

"I mean, why does it take an act of congress for a wealthy man to give his cook a raise?"

"You'll have to ask Mr. Cain," Eberhart said smugly. "As you so rightly pointed out to the cook, *you're asking the wrong person.*"

"Yes, I did say that, and you're right, I will ask Ramsey about it. But there was something else going on in that kitchen. And you're the only one who can explain it. Only you can tell me why seeing Ramsey's discomfort over money made you so happy."

"It did no such thing," Eberhart insisted.

"Come on, I saw the look on your face when Ivy asked for the extra funds. You enjoyed Ramsey's embarrassment. You know something, and you're not letting on."

"That is nonsense," the housekeeper said, crossing her arms over her thin chest. "The only people who would know anything about Mr. Cain's money are Mr. Cain...and Tony Camarella, the accountant for the company."

The housekeeper gave the photographs one last, overly cautious adjustment. She stopped to lift the silver-framed shot of a smiling Holly clutching Ramsey's arm.

"They were a striking couple, don't you think?" Eberhart asked coolly.

"I suppose," Landis said, without much conviction. "Ramsey doesn't look particularly happy."

Again that uneasy feeling that Eberhart was more interested in Mrs. Cain than Mr. Cain prickled along Landis's spine, and the look on the older woman's face as she gazed down at the photo was...rapturous.

"You and Mrs. Cain must have been very close." Landis watched the housekeeper's look fade to nothing.

"No, I came to the house after her untimely death. I never had the pleasure of actually meeting her." Eberhart sighed deeply, and the little warning bells in Landis's head began to clang frantically.

"That's odd. I would've thought you had very deep feelings for her," Landis said, hoping to provoke the woman into talking.

Something wasn't right! The way Eberhart spoke about Holly reminded Landis of the way a teenage girl sighed over the latest Hollywood hunk. It was deep and unnatural and tended to make everyone standing too close more than a little uncomfortable. And Landis was definitely standing too close. But she knew from their conversations that the housekeeper wouldn't give up any information without prodding.

"When *did* you start?"

Eberhart's suspicious expression deepened. "Two month's after Mrs. Cain's tragic death."

"Untimely death." "Tragic death." Why was Holly's death the only point of reference for this woman?

"You speak very fondly of a woman you never met, especially since everyone else didn't like her much," Landis said pointedly.

Eberhart looked down at her from that intimidating height. "As I said before, spend your time doing your job and not gossiping with that old crone."

Landis knew immediately that Eberhart meant Orphy, but how did the housekeeper know that she had spoken to Ramsey's aunt? Was Eberhart spying on her? She decided to push a little harder and tried to suppress the niggling sensations creeping up her spine.

"I don't know if it's just gossip, but I heard that Mrs. Cain could be a real bitch."

Eberhart's face turned white, then a mottled red; her eyes flashed with hatred so sharp Landis wondered for a moment if six feet of utterly furious housekeeper wasn't about to fly into her.

After a moment of nerve-jangling tension, Eberhart seemed to get herself under control. "I warned you about believing everything you hear," she snapped and opened the door that led to the foyer, closing it again with a bang that echoed through the house.

Oh, this is just too weird, Landis thought, staring at the closed door. What had made her so angry? If she hadn't come to work for Ramsey until after Holly's death, why did calling Holly names set Eberhart off?

Landis thought about it a moment, then shook her head in frustration. Everyone in the house acted weird, and

Landis wondered how long it would be before she started to act that way herself.

At least she had a lead on Tony. Now all she needed was a plan. How to get the information from Ramsey's trusted accountant.

She wandered out of the library and, in the kitchen, found Ivy McCreary making up a tray with homemade scones and a pot of coffee.

"Isn't Mr. Cain coming down for lunch?" Landis asked, taking the same seat she'd used the day before.

"No, and he asked for nothing to eat," the cook complained.

Landis inhaled the delicious aroma of homemade chicken soup. "That smells heavenly."

"Is his coffee ready?" Eberhart asked, entering the kitchen, her head held high.

"Yes," Ivy snapped. "Hold your water."

Eberhart didn't even acknowledge Landis, so she cleared her throat and smiled at Eberhart when the woman glanced at her. Eberhart gave her a venomous glare but said nothing. She turned and sailed out of the kitchen with Ramsey's meager tray.

Ivy gave Landis a curious look. "Appears you're on Her Majesty's short list."

"She doesn't like me," Landis acknowledged with feigned disappointment.

"I don't think she'd like anyone who held so much sway over Mr. Cain."

The comment reminded Landis of the salacious innuendo Eberhart had made the previous morning, and she decided there was no time like the present to straighten things out with the cook, especially since Ramsey would most likely handle the whole thing with all the grace of a tornado. She didn't want him being as harsh with Ivy as he'd been with Eberhart.

"I know you all probably thought Mr. Cain and I were...you know." She just couldn't seem to say the word "lovers." "But it's just not true. I didn't meet Mr. Cain until I walked through the front door a couple of days ago. And I don't hold any sway over anyone."

"You got him to come downstairs for lunch. That's more than anyone else—even his aunt—has managed since his wife died."

"Well, be that as it may, there's nothing but a professional relationship between Ramsey and me."

"Orphy's going to be very disappointed," the cook said, filling a bowl with soup and handing it to Landis. "She had her heart set on you saving him."

Sorry to disappoint her, Landis thought. But she couldn't save herself from doing jobs that turned her stomach, much less save Ramsey from whatever demons nipped at his heels.

"Speaking of Orphy, where is she?" Landis asked, hoping to change the subject. The cheerful old woman was just what she needed to brighten this bizarre day. And she was willing to lay money on Orphy's having the answers to some of her questions.

"Off playing bingo at the Wal-Mart," the cook said with a giggle.

"You said something about that before. You're kidding, right?"

"I'm serious," Ivy's eyes twinkled. "Most folks around here are either Catholic or Methodist. Miss Orphy is a bingo-ist. And the Wal-Mart is just one of the many places she attends services. I think she started playing to give herself a reason to leave the house every day. Then she made friends with some of the regulars, and now she's thoroughly hooked on it."

After Landis finished her soup she decided it wouldn't hurt to throw a few questions about the late Holly Cain at Ivy. After all, unlike the smitten Eberhart, Ivy had actually known the woman.

"You said you worked here before Mrs. Cain's death—did you know her very well?"

"As well as anyone downstairs can know anyone upstairs." Ivy poured herself a cup of coffee and sat down across the table from Landis.

It didn't take any prompting at all to get Ivy to talk.

"She was an odd sock, that one," the cook said flatly. "She didn't much like it here. She and Mr. Cain argued about going down to the city constantly. She didn't even like the kind of food I cooked."

"You're kidding!" Landis supplied, egging her on.

"She said it was low-class. Low-class it might be, but it's filling, and I don't hear you complaining."

"And you won't," Landis agreed, pushing her empty soup bowl aside.

"That's the best thanks a cook can get, ya know." Ivy sighed. "Mrs. Cain took to drinking on the sneak and the two of them fought all the more."

"Were you here the night she died?"

"No, more's the pity," the cook's eyes filled with tears. "I was visiting my daughter—she had just had my granddaughter, Sophy. I often wonder if I had been here...if things would have been...different."

This was the second time she had brought someone to tears by dredging up that night. It made the back of her own throat burn.

"The police asked me all about the mister and missus. Did they fight a lot? Did I ever see him hit her? That sort of rubbish. I told them that woman was a hard piece, and if they wanted someone to give them the rope to hang Mr. Cain with they were gonna have to look elsewhere."

"You like Mr. Cain, don't you?"

"I do, and I know what that wife of his was like. Mr. Cain was a good man once upon a time, and God willing, his luck is getting better."

Landis knew that last comment was for her benefit, and she knew that was all Ivy would say. She watched quietly as the cook finished her coffee and cleared the table, and wondered how this man could command so much loyalty from the people around him. And if that explained her own strange feelings about him.

~ * ~

Landis snuck into the office after lunch. She was getting good at sneaking. So good, in fact, that she fantasized someone might put it on her headstone. *Here lies Landis Delaney. World-Class Sneak.*

She crept to his bedroom door and listened. Whatever he was doing in there, he wasn't making a sound.

She had spent the rest of her lunch hour and a long, calming walk around the garden figuring out what to do next. She needed to know why the whole episode about the money had set off those little bells in her head. She doubted if anyone in the house, including Orphy, knew what kind of shape Ramsey's finances were in, and she sure couldn't ask Ramsey.

That left only Tony Camarella. All she needed was a plan to extract the information she needed. If the money facts were good enough, Paula would have her story. She could be out of the house in a matter of minutes, and Ramsey and his heated gaze would be nothing but an unsettling memory.

She knew the angle she needed to use on the accountant: a slightly altered version of the truth. That was fast becoming something else they could chisel on her headstone. *Her life was a slightly altered version of the truth.*

She tiptoed across the office and into her bedroom, found the cell-phone, and closed herself up in the privacy of her little bathroom. It took her a moment to remember the number for the Pittsburgh office.

An efficient voice came on the line. "Good afternoon, Cain-Dunham."

"Yes, this is Ramsey Cain's office for Tony Camarella in accounting."

"That's extension 398. I'll connect you."

The voice was gone, replaced by an instrumental version of the Rolling Stone's "Satisfaction." After a few minutes a hearty laugh came through the line "You're getting downright impatient in your old age, ma man."

"Mr. Camarella, this is Landis Delaney, Mr. Cain's assistant."

"Well," he said, surprised. "Sorry for the "old age" crack. From what I hear, that doesn't apply to you."

Oh, that was a loaded statement. She wanted to demand what he had heard about her but thought better of it. She had to stay focused on her task.

"Ramsey asked that I call you and find out if that money had been transferred yet." she said, her voice as casual as she could make it.

"Ramsey told you about this?" Tony asked, sounding skeptical.

"Yes, he's told me all about it," she assured him. "How is it coming?"

"Okay. I dumped the last of his communications stock this morning. The broker is handling the transfer of the money, but can cut a check any time he wants it."

Landis waited, hoping Tony would be as willing to volunteer information as Ivy and Orphy had, but the other end of the phone grew conspicuously quiet. Landis scrambled for something to say.

This is a friend of Ramsey's, she told herself. What would appeal to a good friend who only wanted to help?

"I'm really worried about this, Tony," she said sweetly. "It is all right to call you Tony, isn't it?"

"Yeah, sure. Tony's fine," he said, his voice now filled with concern. "And, listen, don't worry. Your job's secure."

There was a definite Pittsburgh twang to his voice. He pronounced it "sic-ure" instead of "see-cure." This man, like Bridget, Orphy, and Ivy, was loyal. Despite the suspicion of murder that hung over him, it seemed that everyone who knew Ramsey remained firmly behind him.

"No, it isn't my job," she insisted. "It's Ramsey...I mean, Mr. Cain."

That was good, she told herself. Insinuate a closer relationship than there is. She sounded so sincere, so concerned. She made herself sick.

"Don't worry about Ramsey," Tony said, and his voice had grown suddenly softer, more sympathetic. "That thick hide of his covers a pretty tough interior. No matter how close the wolf gets to the door, Ramsey knows how to fight it off. Once the mall project gets underway and the money starts coming in to the company Ramsey will turn that Midas touch of his back on his investments and be back on his feet in no time."

Wolves. Back on his feet. *Specifics, man, I need specifics.* Aloud, she said. "Well, that's reassuring, but will the mall project be enough?"

"Believe me, even a company like this one can be saved by all this monster mall money."

"But does it really need to be saved?" she asked, throwing a hint of desperation into her voice for good measure.

"Ramsey has kept the coffers at a workable level. Granted, it has cost him most of his personal fortune, but, hey, like the man says, 'It's only money.'"

Only money! Landis thought. At last estimation, Ramsey had been worth a cool eighteen million. Surely it all couldn't have been swallowed up in three years. "So, you're confident I don't need to look for another job?" Landis asked for one last chance at a clear answer.

"Relax," Tony said, sounding genuinely uncertain. "If anyone can pull this off, it's Ramsey. As long as those lawyers stay happy, all is well."

"Good!" she said, maybe too enthusiastically. "I'm...glad. Well, it was good talking to you, Tony."

"Yeah, have that ogre bring you to the big city someday. I'd like to get a look at the lady who could make the Ramrod tow the mark."

Again with the Ramrod, Landis thought. "I'd like that. Bye."

She closed the phone, breaking the connection, and sagged against the bathroom door.

Finally, just what she needed—a story.

~ * ~

Landis strolled into the office and slid into her seat as quietly as she could. She didn't want to disturb him if he still slept. He had looked very tired the day before. More than likely, his bad mood the previous morning could be blamed on a lack of sleep, and the lack of sleep on his lousy money situation. The puzzle made sense now that she had the pieces.

She had to wait until evening when Paula got home, since she was under orders not to call the anchorwoman at the station. She would give her the story and be out of here in a heartbeat. Until then, it wouldn't hurt to clean up Ramsey's computer files for him—or for the next lucky girl that came to work for him.

Oh, why did that cause a little flutter under her ribs? Would he hire someone else? She would make up some excuse to get out the door, probably one even dumber than the lies that got her in the door, and be gone forever.

Would Ramsey scratch his head, shrug his shoulders, and call Gaiser for a replacement? Or would he feel so betrayed that he'd never again trust another woman? First Holly, then Landis Delaney. Maybe it would be the last time he trusted anyone.

Damn, there was that flutter again.

She didn't have a chance to give it any more thought before Ramsey's bedroom door exploded open.

Landis nearly dove under her desk. "What—"

"Don't say a word," he roared, crossing the room in long strides. "What did you hope to find?"

She panicked. Tony must have literally called him as soon as she hung up the phone.

"Answer me!" he shouted. He stood over her like a giant bird of prey, and all the things she had heard about him, all the rumors and suspicions, congealed into a lump of terror in the pit of her stomach. Fear clogged her throat, shutting off her words, even when she opened her mouth to speak.

His breath came in sporadic bursts. The muscles in his lean cheeks twitched, giving him a slightly demonic expression. "Well?"

"You said not to say a word," she said meekly.

That full sensual mouth, the one that had kissed her, thinned into a hard line, and his voice sounded as brittle as flint. "As a rule, I find your sense of humor enchanting, but not now. Don't try to charm me with those big blue eyes. Just tell me what you hoped to accomplish going behind my back to Tony."

Think, Landis! she repeated again and again in her head. "I only wanted to straighten out your personal finances." She said it softly, more to see how it would sound than anything else.

He narrowed his eyes. "You what?"

"It's my job to handle these things for you. Things like personal finances." *Oh, that sounded so reasonable.* "You seemed upset when Ivy asked you for the money, and I thought perhaps this is one of those things I should handle for you."

She waited while Ramsey stared at her, the thin line of his lips relaxing a fraction.

It's working, she thought, and I didn't even have to tell much of a lie that time. It really was a personal assistant's job to handle personal accounts, and he *had* been upset when he spoke to Ivy. All right, she had left a lot out, but she looked into those angry gray eyes and couldn't bring herself to say anything more.

~ * ~

Ramsey stared into her serious face. A million questions shot through his mind, none of which pleased him. How the hell had she gotten hold of Tony? While his instincts about women had never been very good and he suspected she *had* only been trying to help, something about the situation felt wrong—very wrong.

"Who told you to mess with the household accounts?" he snapped. "That's my accountant's job."

"I told you. I thought it part of my duties. I'm your personal assistant, remember?" She made a beeline for the relative safety of the other side of the room. "This sort of thing falls under my job description," she added warily.

"I decide what your job is, and what it is not." He cursed to himself, glad she'd moved away once she actually had. Her soft blue eyes, her slightly parted pink mouth, even wearing that terrified expression, worked on his anger. He found it utterly remarkable that suddenly he *didn't* have the desire to fight with her. Oh, he had all kinds of desires when it came to Landis, and he needed her to stay out of his finances, but he didn't want to yell at her any more. He didn't want to lose his temper, and he didn't want to push her away.

What was wrong with him? God knew he had a right to be angry. She had gone behind his back, talked to Tony, and, he suspected, wouldn't have said a word to him if Tony hadn't called. He had certainly been angry enough then.

But standing over Landis seeing fear and worry cloud her face and watching the way she chewed the corner of her lip had drained the fight right out of him. Unfortunately, it didn't touch those other desires still churning just beneath the surface.

He stalked past her to the window, and the soft scent of her hair teased at his senses. He made a conscious effort to put distance between them.

Good heavens, Landis thought. He's pacing again. A trapped expression had entered his eyes.

"I suppose you know everything," he said sharply.

"Yes," she said, stunning herself more than Ramsey. "I heard everything when you were on the phone yesterday, but Tony assured me this mall complex would turn things around for the company He also told me you were putting your own money into saving the business."

"You could have asked me," he said.

"I'm sorry," she said, taking the opportunity to join him at the window. "Next time I will."

"There won't be a next time, Landis," he said, but the sternness in his voice didn't reach his eyes.

"Are you firing me?" Landis looked up into those eyes and felt lost.

He turned toward the window. "Not this time."

"I don't understand what the problem is. Your company looks pretty good to me," she said.

"After Holly's death and the bad publicity, the bigger accounts stopped coming," he said, and his voice had that distant, haunted tone that melted her heart. "The mall project is the first contract of any size I've had since my name became synonymous with Bluebeard's."

Landis flinched. She'd called him an upscale Bluebeard, and hearing the words come back to her stung. "So you put your own money into the company accounts."

"Cain-Dunham is a huge organization with over fifty full-time employees and twice as many part-time and subcontractors. The work was no longer there because of me. I couldn't let everything I'd worked for, everything Bridget and Tony and all the others had worked for, fall away to nothing. I began filtering my money in shortly after the coroner's inquest. I worked out the arrangements with Tony. At first, I thought the work would pick up, but as time went on I saw my own pockets withering. I cut back everywhere I could. I even had to lay off some of the part-time workers. With most construction starts down, I let them think it was a normal fluctuation in the business."

"But if things are so bad," Landis asked, cautiously touching his arm. "Why did you hire me?"

"I sold the family cabin in Latrobe and dumped a few stocks. It gave me a bit of breathing room. Everything I have is riding on this mall complex. And I've had so much trouble. I need someone I can count on, an assistant to make this project go smoothly. I need you."

Landis had listened to his story with a growing pain somewhere in the region of her heart. He counted on her—and a woman who wanted to ruin him firmly controlled her. She moved her hand away, suddenly more ashamed of herself than she had ever thought she could be.

Ramsey caught her before she pulled completely away. "There's a check on my desk for Mrs. McCreary. Tell her to get whatever she needs to fill the pantry. Tell her I'd like some of her wonderful peach pies. I've missed them. Don't mention any of this to Orphy. All she has is Uncle Maury's pension, but she'd probably insist on paying rent or something."

"I'll take care of everything," Landis said softly, and felt him gently squeeze her hand before he let her go.

"And don't you worry either," he said, walking slowly to the door. "This will work out. It has to."

Landis closed the door to her bedroom and leaned against it. She hated herself, and she hated what she had to do next.

~ * ~

Edward threw the cup he carried against the wall, shattering it. "Damn the luck!" he shouted into the empty attic. It was one thing to have that irritating woman under foot, but to have her so in control of Cain was more than he could bear.

It had taken months of work to learn what little he had about Ramsey, and to see how quickly the little redhead had gained the man's favor disgusted him. He had already decided that Landis Delaney would pay for her disrespect to his beloved sister's memory. But this closeness with Cain he had not anticipated. His small but substantial control over the house, so long overlooked, would no doubt be undermined. And all his plans for Cain would suffer.

He had to do something...but what?

Should he kill her?

Almost as quickly as the thought came, he pushed it aside. If Miss Delaney were found dead there would be an investigation. His position was too precarious to withstand close scrutiny.

Of course, he reasoned, if a death were investigated wouldn't the authorities first look at the man already suspected of killing a woman?

He smiled at his reflection.

They would suspect Ramsey.

Edward took a sheet of paper from his desk and began to make notes. How? When? So many things had to be considered when laying out a plot to do murder, especially when the guilt must fall on someone else. But it was possible.

Finally, the means to his revenge appeared right at his fingertips.

Eight

Landis pulled the phone from the suitcase and opened it. She told herself she had no choice. Paula insisted on something, anything, that she could use in her report about Ramsey.

Passing this information to Paula was better than telling her any of the personal things she had learned. She wouldn't mention that Holly had been a drunk, or that an aging aunt, an old girlfriend-cum-business partner, and a few people who worked for him were the only real friends Ramsey had left in the world. She wouldn't mention that he lived like a character in an old gothic novel, isolated in his dark mansion.

Once she had Paula on the phone, Landis decided, she would only tell her that Ramsey was having a minor cash-flow problem, and even that she would carefully play down.

"Paula Rice's office, please," Landis told the switchboard operator. "Tell her it's the Mole-woman from Armstrong County."

Paula had warned her not to call the office, but the heck with Paula. Landis wanted this over, before she lost her lunch.

"Why are you calling me here?"

"I have your damn story," Landis snapped.

"Well, that was quick," Paula said tartly. "So, what is Mr. Cain up to that has you sounding so tense?"

"Money," Landis said, pressing a hand to her roiling stomach. For a moment she was certain she was going to be sick. She promised herself that no matter what happened in her life she would never again subject herself to this sort of thing.

"Money?" Paula sounded vaguely uninterested.

"Actually, the lack of it," Landis sighed.

"You're out of money?" Paula questioned with a huff.

"Not me." She pulled the phone away for a second and made a face at it. "God, you're dumb. Ramsey. Ramsey is almost out of money."

There it was. She had done it. She had lowered herself to the level of Paula Rice and her type. She was definitely going to be sick.

After a long pause, Paula barked a short laugh. "Is that it? I swear I'll fire you if you don't come up with something more interesting…and quick. Do I have to remind you that your job depends on this? No one cares about money. They want sex, murder, drugs, insanity, something that claws at the soul, not the pocketbook."

Soul! What the hell did this woman know about soul? The man Paula wanted to publicly execute for a second time had more soul in his little finger than—

Landis cut the thought off. Her blood pressure had already shot through the roof, and her stomach hurt like hell. She would gain nothing by ranting to herself.

"I can only give you what I know," Landis said, taking deep breaths. "If that isn't good enough then maybe you *should* fire me."

She slammed shut the little phone.

Was she kidding? It wasn't enough. Paula wanted more. But there wasn't any more. She had given her everything there was. Did all Paula's raving mean that nothing would come of the information after all?

It didn't help—she still felt like a traitor, and a spy. And even a hot shower couldn't wash away the feeling that she had dirtied herself with what she'd done.

Landis tossed and turned all night. Nightmare images filled her restless sleep, in which she found herself again at the foot of the stairs where Holly had died. Instead of Holly Cain it was Ramsey lying bloodied and battered on the tile. Someone in the dream accused her of killing him. All she could do was plead that she hadn't meant to hurt anyone. She had awakened to the sound of her own voice begging forgiveness.

Trembling, she sat up and looked nervously around. Had she heard someone in the shadows of the room? The pale moonlight revealed nothing. "Is someone there?" she asked, her tone too weak to intimidate anyone.

"Why do I always feel that someone is watching me?" she asked the shadows. She settled back onto her pillow and closed her eyes. In a matter of moments her breathing was again deep and regular.

Ramsey stepped from a dark corner of the bedroom. He hadn't meant to frighten her, but the sounds he heard coming from her room had drawn him to her. He'd been worried that something was wrong and had broken the promise he had made to himself to stay out of her bedroom.

She had called out to someone, pleading with them to forgive her. Over and over she had said she was sorry, that she hadn't meant to hurt *him*. But who *he* was remained a mystery.

"What's troubling you, beautiful?" he whispered. "What can I do to help?"

Her only reply was a deep sigh.

~ * ~

Morning found Landis in the office, alone as usual. It was just as well—she needed time to think, and she had to decide what to do next. Ramsey's confession and her double-cross had taken her nowhere, and she still had the little problem of trying to keep her job at the station to think about. Luckily, there were lots of things around the office that needed a real secretarial touch.

She faxed a copy of the blueprints Ramsey had worked on the night before to the office in Pittsburgh and, thanks to the fact that Ramsey carried the same on-line service as the station, checked her e-mail. She had planned to leave a message for Melba but found that, as usual, her assistant was one step ahead of her. There was a message waiting.

The message read: *I have what you asked for. Let me know if there is anything else. A. M.*

Landis smiled. A. M. Always, Melba. It was the way they had signed messages at work that they didn't want connected to their names. In the politically-charged atmosphere of television news it was important never to write anything down with a name connected to it. It was important to know who to trust.

Melba was the trustworthiest person in the world. She had proved herself over and over. Now Landis counted on her to help get her out of this situation, and, as usual, Melba was right on the ball.

Landis downloaded the information Melba had been able to pull together: a file on Ramsey, much more complete than the dossier Paula had given her to study, and a file on both Orphy Salankewietz and Ivy McCreary. At the bottom of the transmission was a note.

I haven't been able to find anything on Alison Eberhart. But I haven't given up. A. M.

She smiled as she read the last part. It would never have occurred to her that Melba would give up.

The printer came on with a click and a hum, and Landis printed out the information. As the section on Orphy began to feed through the outdated printer, Ramsey opened his bedroom door. Landis shot out of her seat and placed herself between him and printer.

"I didn't mean to startle you," he said.

Landis recognized that the dark mood which had gripped him the day before had not completely dissipated. "I didn't expect you," she answered, her breath in her throat. That was a lie—she had been afraid the moment the printer started that he would be joining her. She marveled at her bad luck.

"Did you sleep well?" he asked. His intense gaze fixed itself on her as he sat down at his drafting table.

The memory of her bad dreams, fueled by her smarting conscience and everything that had happened the night before, clawed at her. She hadn't slept well, and she had awakened again to the unsettling feeling that someone had been watching her.

"As well as I can in a strange bed," she said.

"What's going on this morning?"

"Just interesting things on-line: a recipe for chocolate brownies, a copy of a poem by Maya Angelou, and gossip from my friends."

"It's nice to see all that technology is being put to good use." He straightened his vest, and Landis took a moment to look him over. As always, he wore dark and sober clothes—black slacks and a gray shirt. The vest was one she had not seen before, black brocade with diamond shapes woven into the fabric in shades of gray and shot through with silver.

"I have to work up the electrical service on this set of prints," he said, taking his seat. "So I won't need your help this afternoon. Why don't you take the day off and come in around four?"

"Are you trying to get rid of me?" she asked, looking nervously over her shoulder at the printer that had almost finished.

"Nothing of the sort." He glanced at her out of the corner of his eye. "I'm getting rid of a distraction."

"A lesser woman wouldn't like being referred to as a distraction," she pointed out.

"A lesser woman wouldn't be a distraction," he returned.

Landis took a moment to think about that. It was a compliment. She was about to call him on it when he continued.

"Go on," he urged. "Visit with Ivy or follow my aunt to one of her bingo games."

"Fine," she said, taking the last sheet of paper from the printer. She wasn't wild about the idea of her background checks on Ramsey and his family lying around the office anyway. This would give her time to take them to her room, read over them, and secret them away. She didn't have time to get her things together, however, before the phone rang.

Bridget, on the other end, exchanged pleasantries with Landis that sounded forced. Landis gave the phone to Ramsey and waited. A sense of dread filled her. Something else had gone wrong. Bridget's voice had been wound tighter than piano wire, and Ramsey's face grew darker and more intense by the second.

"Oh, for the love of—" Ramsey roared, coming off his chair. "What does he want? I've included everything that man wanted. What did he say, word for word?"

Landis watched him pace the office in front of the windows and wondered why seeing him so distressed upset her.

"What does he mean...not open enough?" he snapped. "The design was agreed on three weeks ago. Changing it now will only set the project back farther. Tell him this will raise the cost of design by fifty percent and any further changes will cost double."

Landis slid the computer printout into her desk. Something told her that her afternoon off had just been canceled. She opened the large cabinet where Ramsey kept his blueprint paper and placed it on his drafting table. From the files she got a copy of the mall layout.

She called on the intercom while Ramsey finished his call and asked Ivy to bring up a pot of strong coffee and several of her scones. So much for her afternoon off.

Ramsey shook his head as he sat at the drafting table. "Ludwig wants the layout to be 'more bright and open.' He had a woman in his office who gave him some kind of mystic Oriental reading, and now he thinks everything about the design is too constrictive."

"Feng shui," Landis said. She had researched it for a piece only a few weeks earlier and had been interested in the idea. Of course, her little office back at the station was too cramped to apply anything she learned, but she had moved a few things around her apartment to make the space more appealing, and she had noticed that it worked.

"It's the art of making space more harmonious," she explained.

He gave her a dubious stare. "Well, now my space is less harmonious. I'd like to feng shui him."

He scowled at the blueprints as though he could change them through sheer force of will. She told herself to leave him alone, but he looked so grim that she wandered across the room to glance over his shoulder. It took a moment for her to understand what she saw. The lines crisscrossing the blue paper seemed to have no rhyme or reason. She concentrated on the diagram, and in a flash the picture came to her. The lines made sense, and if she remembered what she had learned about feng shui she could see why the lawyer had been unhappy.

"What is that look about?" Ramsey asked, gazing at her, a frown creasing his handsome brow.

"It's lovely..."

"But...?"

"But...it is a little tight."

He slid away from the desk and gave her a hard glare. "Tight?" he snapped.

"Well, that was what the lawyer didn't like about it, right? It isn't open enough."

"Excuse me, how many buildings have you designed?" he asked, an edge of sarcasm in his tone.

"None!" she fired back, and with equal derision asked, "And how many malls have you shopped in lately?" She turned to her own desk.

What had she been thinking, sticking her nose in his blueprints? She should be shut up in her safe little bathroom, studying the files Melba had sent her.

He appeared to be thinking about what she'd said. He looked from the prints to Landis, who pretended not to notice his confused expression.

"You're right," he said after a while.

"Excuse me?" Landis asked, as innocently as she could.

"I haven't shopped in a mall since...college."

"Gee, did they have malls back then?"

"Very funny," he said, answering her smile with his own. "Come and take a look at these. Tell me what you think."

He gave her his chair but stayed close. Landis found it hard to concentrate with him standing so near. She was aware of was his presence—aware of the sensation of heat and anxious energy that flooded her bloodstream.

"Well," he prompted.

"At Christmas time, especially the day after Thanksgiving, it will be hard to maneuver through these passages with arms full of packages. Can you open this up and try to face the shops around a wide area, maybe a place with a fountain or benches? There should be several places where shoppers can rest and catch their breath."

The current plans had the center of the mall focused on a stage where special events could be held. It was very nice and would be a special draw for a mall complex, but it would make the simple act of shopping a pain in the neck.

"I hate it when I need something from Wal-Mart, and I have to push past a million people standing around watching a tiny tots' beauty pageant. It's even worse at Christmas Imagine...you're desperate to get to the stores because you left all your shopping until the twenty-second, and all you see is a sea of people waiting to sit their kids on Santa's knee. It's aggravating. Believe me!"

He leaned over her shoulder. "What...if...I..." He made a few quick slashes to the blueprint, opening the center to better through traffic.

"That's better, but what about this?" She picked up a drafting pencil and looked at him for permission to doodle on his masterpiece.

"Go ahead," he said, leaning closer to watch her.

She wished he wasn't so close. He had a hand on the back of her chair, and the side of his broad chest brushed intimately against her arm.

Landis took a deep breath and drew a large circle around a smaller circle in the center. Off the larger circle like spokes from a wheel the stores would radiate, all sharing a front view of the fountains and benches.

"Maybe a dome over the fountain to fill the space with sunlight, lots of plants and those mall trees."

"Mall trees?"

"Yeah, the palmy kind, you know." She gave him a devilish grin. "Man, you weren't kidding. It *has* been a long time since you were in a mall."

He took the pencil from her hand and turned her circles in to almost perfect octagons, giving the stores angular fronts. "This is very good, Landis," he said, his voice smooth as velvet in her ear. He leaned down next to her chair, putting himself at eye level, and Landis's stomach fluttered.

"Now, close your eyes," he said in almost a whisper.

Landis narrowed her eyes suspiciously. Ramsey slid his hand onto her nape, sending a surge of heat through her.

~ * ~

The moment he touched her a jolt, like an electric shock, coursed from him to her and back. He had meant to reassure her, but now all he felt was her warmth, the soft crackle of energy that flowed between them, the satiny texture of her skin, and the silky brush of her auburn curls on his hand.

He watched her lashes flutter closed. "Now, picture in your mind's eye what you described." He kept his voice deliberately soft, a hot whisper in her ear. "See the fountain and the benches."

A smile turned the corners of her mouth up, and he knew she could see it.

"See the trees, the walkway with its green park benches and beds of brightly colored flowers. Now, look around at the stores. What stores do you see there?"

Her smile broadened. "Waldenbooks. The Body Shop. Maybe Victoria's Secret."

"It sounds wonderful," he murmured.

He'd forgotten what it was like to imagine something you created for the first time. Now Landis's rapturous expression reminded him why he had wanted to build things in the first place.

And reminded him how badly he wanted to kiss her. He had teased her once that she was a temptation, but now the joke was on him. She did tempt him, nearly to the edge of his resistance.

~ * ~

When Landis opened her eyes she found Ramsey's face a few inches from her own. The vulnerability she had seen there before was gone, replaced by a hunger that had etched itself in the hard lines and sharp angles of his features. He studied her face, her eyes, her cheeks, her lips, the contour of her jaw. And she knew that no one had ever looked at her so intensely, as though committing her to his memory forever.

As he moved closer still, Landis parted her lips and gave herself over to the kiss. Ramsey pushed past any token resistance she might have offered and claimed her lips, leaving her weak with wanting more.

He tightened his hold on her and slowly stood, taking her out of the seat and drawing her against his body. That perfect body. She reached out to him for support and found the hard slope of his shoulders. Her hands traced the fine linen of his shirt around his back and she pulled herself tighter against him.

He left her mouth and nuzzled the sensitive place under her ear. A sound between a moan and a whimper came from her, bringing his mouth back to hers.

And his hands... He slid one hand from her neck down her back, tipping her slightly backward. His other hand skimmed the length of her body. He caught her behind the knee, drawing her leg up and around his hip, fitting her perfectly to him.

She was suddenly so happy she had chosen to wear a skirt that morning. He slipped his hand beneath the hem and snaked it along her thigh.

~ * ~

Oh, merciful God! he thought. She had thighs like silk. If the Lord had created anything more perfect, Ramsey doubted he could bear knowing about it. Landis returned his kiss, answering his desperate need with groans and soft sounds that only pushed him to take more of the sweetness she offered. She ran her hands the length of his back, as though frantic to do something.

He cupped his hand on the soft curve of her shapely derriere and pressed her tighter to his aching loins. He thought he would go mad if he didn't touch her. He lifted her onto the edge of the drafting table and pressed his lips again to her ear. "Landis," he whispered in a voice too raspy to be his own.

Her answer was a throaty hum that urged him on.

"I want you," he said. "I need you. I—"

"Have me," she groaned.

Leaving the warmth of her thighs, his fingers tugged the hem of her shirt from her waistband and fumbled with the bottom button. The first came off in his fingers, and Landis wiggled away. For a frightening moment he thought she wanted him to stop. Instead, she pulled herself up enough to balance and pushed him back far enough to reach between them. In a fraction of the time he would have needed she had opened the buttons on her shirt and had moved to those on his vest.

There was a moment of confusion on his face and then utter relief that she was not pushing him away.

"Come here," she said, answering his unspoken question.

The dying voice of her logic pleaded with her to think about this. To remember who this was. Who she was.

A rumble of a laugh started in Ramsey's chest. But he had pulled her to him again and slid his hand over one breast, and the voice in her head became a strangled whisper. Landis strained against his hand, and the nipple beneath her bra pebbled wantonly.

"Are you sure?" he asked.

"Are you kidding?" she gasped.

She had managed to open some of the buttons on his shirt, enough to slip her hand inside. It wasn't enough. She pushed him back and worked the buttons, at the same time wiggling herself against the leg she now straddled.

"I don't want to push you," he said as Landis finally pulled the shirt off his shoulders.

"Don't talk." She drew him down to her. She wanted to feel his hot skin against hers. "Talking leads to thinking. I don't want to think."

He kissed her again, harder and more demanding. Landis buried her hands in his hair, letting the heavy silk slip through her fingers, and she knew there was no going back.

Ramsey felt the soft rasp of her lace bra against his chest and the provocative grind of her heated loins against his. It was going to happen. He tried to reason against the sheer impossibility of the situation. He had gone from veritable monk to randy adolescent, and all it had taken was the nearness, the soft sigh, and the smile of this remarkable woman.

And she wasn't turning him away. She wasn't cursing him or fighting to escape. Hell, she wanted this as much as he did, which only made him want her more.

His heart hammered in his ears as he slid both hands under the hem of her raised skirt to the edge of her silk panties. Landis lifted herself slightly, and he was able to loop his fingers in the delicate elastic that held them snug to the curve of her hips.

The hammering in his head became a pounding, and the pounding came with a voice that called his name.

He froze.

Landis glared up at him. "What now?" she asked impatiently.

"Listen," he whispered.

"Ramsey." It was Orphy's voice, and it came from the other side of the door.

"Damn," Ramsey growled, and Landis sagged back onto the drafting table.

"For heaven's sake, let me in!" his aunt shouted.

By the time Ramsey had buttoned his shirt and vest and opened the door Landis had pulled herself together and was seated at her desk.

Orphy eyed them suspiciously. "What took so long?"

Ramsey mumbled something, and Landis fought a smile.

"I never thought drawing buildings would be so engrossing that you couldn't hear an old woman beating at the door."

"I can hear you now," he grumbled.

"My car isn't feeling well," Orphy said, ignoring his testy remark. "Ivy is going to bring me back from the garage in your car but I won't have any way to get to the senior center this morning."

"What's going on at the senior center?" he asked, though at the moment he couldn't have cared less.

"It's Thursday," she said, as though he should have some idea of its significance. "The Social Security checks come out, and the old men come to the center to play poker."

"So?" her nephew said, and Landis grinned at his impatience.

"Well, it's the best time to meet men," Orphy said, giving him a haughty look. "They have the funds to take you to lunch or buy you flowers."

He sighed and shook his head as Landis laughed. "Fine. You can take my car."

"I hate your car, it's too big." Orphy turned her attention to Landis. "You have a cute little car. Could I borrow it, my dear?"

Surprised, Landis hesitated only a moment before reaching for her purse to get her keys. "Of course."

She handed Orphy the keys and Ramsey's aunt give him a conspiratorial wink. "I know it seems foolish for an old woman to go out looking for...*companionship*, but I don't have the luxury of having it sleeping next door to me," Orphy said as she left the room.

Landis glanced at Ramsey, who only looked uncomfortable and then looked away.

~ * ~

An hour later, Landis picked up the phone when it rang, and her face grew suddenly tense "Yes, I'm Landis Delaney. Yes, that's my car, but I... Oh, my God, is she all right? Yes, of course, we'll be right there."

Ramsey had come off his seat, crossed the room to stand at her side. "What is it?"

"We have to go to the hospital," Landis said in a deceptively calm voice. "Orphy's had an accident."

~ * ~

Edward cursed under his breath. The car accident had been meant for Landis, not that meddling old hag. The least the old biddy could have done was have the decency to die, he thought with a snide grin.

Why had his plan failed? He had been ever-so-careful, cutting the brake lines in a spot unlikely to be noticed, collecting the thick fluid so as not to leave a single drop to mark the driveway. Of course, he had not counted on the old woman's using Landis's car.

It had been too elaborate, too outside his realm of expertise. After all, he was an artist, not a mechanic. He would be even more vigilant next time. Stick with what he knew.

But what?

He understood acting, and acting was symbolism. One of his acting coaches had told him that years ago. He understood symbolism. He understood an eye for an eye. He knew that Ramsey had killed his beloved sister in this house—and that was where Landis Delaney should die.

The stairs. Holly had died on the stairs. And on the stairs would be where he would take his revenge. Ramsey would know, then, that it was Holly reaching out from the grave to snatch away his happiness and his life.

Edward smiled at his reflection, that evil smile he liked so well. This time there would be no mistake.

Nine

Orphy rested as comfortably as possible without a game of bingo to distract her. Despite the car's airbag she had suffered a concussion in the crash, and the doctor was having trouble regulating her mild case of diabetes. He assured her the problem was the result of the stress caused by the accident. A few days in the hospital were in order.

Orphy soon began to complain, and Ramsey decided she was well on her way to recovery. Landis's car, however, had not fared so well. The mechanic who had towed it out of the cow pasture said it would take a lot of work. Landis wasn't concerned about the loss—insurance would cover it—but she wanted to know what had gone wrong and why the brakes on a new car had failed. The mechanic thought the brake lines had been cut, but offered to give it a full autopsy and call her with the results.

Landis could read the worry in the fine lines around Ramsey's mouth. "Your aunt's a very strong woman," she said to break the silence.

"She's not as strong as she thinks. She needs to slow down before—" he broke off, and Landis knew he was afraid to even suggest something might happen to Orphy if she kept up her pace.

"Well, I wouldn't want to be the person who had to slow her down." She thought about her own grandmother and before she realized it was talking about her. "...nothing stops her. She's eighty-one and still drives this beat-up old Buick. My father tried to get her something smaller, easier to park, but she refuses. She said she wasn't wasting her money on a car that would outlast her."

"I think your grandmother and my aunt would get along famously," Ramsey observed. "I can't wait to meet her."

"She likes dark-haired men. She'll love you." Too late Landis realized what she'd said and struggled to find a graceful way to cover her tracks. "I mean..."

"If she's anything like her granddaughter, I'm sure we'll get along fine."

He smiled at her, but Landis was suddenly struck dumb with fright. She had spoken about her family, her personal life. It was just one of the many things she had told herself not to do. She didn't want to care for Ramsey Cain, and she did not want to let Ramsey get close enough to care about her. And now she had talked to him on a personal level, letting the memory of his kisses distract her. She was getting too close, close enough that her lies might become obvious.

The rest of the way home Landis said nothing and tried to decide just when she had lost control of the situation.

She stole a sidelong glance at Ramsey, at his beautiful profile, and her stomach clenched. Even now she wanted to reach out to him, to kiss that little indentation in his cheek.

The thought struck her that maybe she had only been deluding herself. Maybe she had never had control in the first place.

~ * ~

The next morning Ramsey left a note in the office telling Landis he had to work on the new design for the mall and that she could have the afternoon off. Landis called Orphy, listened to a graphic depiction of the meals she was forced to eat and promised to send Ivy in with something decent.

She felt sorry for Orphy, the soul of independence. That she had to be pent up in a hospital room must be torture. And Landis still didn't know why. She had to know what had happened to the car.

She looked around the quiet office and realized the rest of the afternoon was her own.

A little later, dressed in a bathing suit she had never worn before, Landis stretched out on a lounger in the beautiful pool with the hot sun on her skin and the cool water on her back, relaxing. Or at least she intended to give it one hell of a try.

However, every time she closed her eyes Ramsey's face appeared in her mind. The memory of his hungry and demanding kisses washed away all other thoughts—her concerns for Orphy, her curiosity about her car—and brought a heated flush to her skin. Remembering her equally desperate responses made her edgy and warm.

What had she been thinking?

Obviously, nothing, she chided herself. She had been lost in the feel of his hands and the rasp of his breath on her flesh. And if not for Orphy's interruption she would have...

She didn't finish the thought. She knew exactly what would have happened, and she was certain it would have been wonderful.

Don't even think that, her conscience warned. If she had made love with Ramsey it would change everything. It would make betraying him impossible. It would make her job at the station nothing more than a faded memory. Then, for just a moment, she wondered why that didn't frighten her as much as it had before.

Lust, her conscience insisted. She was so overwhelmed with lust for that man she couldn't even think straight.

She took a sip of iced tea without opening her eyes. Despite her dark sunglasses, her eyes were tired and overly sensitive to the light, probably because of lack of sleep. She blamed some of her restlessness at night on her guilty conscience, but she knew it was mostly because of Ramsey. He drew her into his dark world—and she had let herself be drawn in, becoming a night person. The shadows, the secrets, the mysteries had become too much a part of her life.

Everything now seemed so complicated. She worried that her feelings for Ramsey, her fears about losing her job, and all the lies had become a jumble she couldn't reason her way through. And if she didn't figure it out soon she wondered if it would consume her.

~ * ~

On the second floor of the new west wing Ramsey stood at the Palladian window in his bedroom.

She looks so relaxed, he thought.

Landis certainly didn't look as though a need for him was slowly driving her insane. She floated around the pool on one of the loungers that had long ago been forgotten by the family, dressed in the smallest red-plaid bikini he'd ever seen. She sipped a drink through a straw and, without a care in the world, trailed her long, shapely legs in the water.

Ramsey, on the other hand, gripped the window frame, convinced that if he let go he would crumble to the floor, a mass of throbbing frustration. He stared at the water lapping around her thighs, and beads of sweat broke out on his upper lip. Sunlight sparkled in her damp hair, and his stomach knotted. She reached for the bottle of sunblock, and he finally pushed away from the window.

Out of the office, through the hall, and down the stairs, he stepped into the back yard before she had finished rubbing the white liquid into the soft skin of her upper thigh.

Ramsey said nothing. He stood at the side of the pool and watched.

~ * ~

Landis was aware of his presence long before she opened her eyes, yet she jumped slightly and had to steady her glass of ice tea.

Dressed entirely in black, he looked as out-of-place standing next to the pool as she would look sitting in a boardroom in her bathing suit. She slid her dark glasses to the end of her nose and squinted up at him. "I thought you had work to do."

"I couldn't ignore the view."

Wearing only a bikini, she felt vulnerable. She slipped off the lounger and under the water. When she emerged at the other side of the pool he was there, waiting for her, holding her robe in his hard, elegant hands. She stepped out of the water, and he slipped the warm terry cloth over her shoulders. His knuckles brushed her neck. The touch became a caress, and as she turned to face him, she found herself in his embrace.

Damn, she had promised herself she wouldn't do this again. But his touch was more than she could resist and the feel of his mouth, hot and demanding, made it easy to forget all those promises.

"I missed you," he said against her neck, trailing kisses down her throat. "I couldn't work with you out here."

"I distracted you again." She laughed at the way he tickled her earlobe.

"Come into the house. We have unfinished business to take care of." His voice was soft and seductive. He took her hand and urged her toward the house.

She followed him as far as the garden. She could no longer ignore the insistent voice of her conscience. "About that unfinished business," she said, pulling out of his grip.

He stopped, turned, and fixed her with a suspicious gaze. "Yes?"

"I think we should give it more thought." Her voice sounded less than convincing. Even she wondered if she really meant it.

"I thought you didn't want to think," he reminded her, slipping a hand beneath the edge of her open robe.

His fiery touch melted the hard edges of her resistance "I know...I—I said that," she stammered. "But I *have* thought about it."

He cursed under his breath, then gave her a thoroughly dejected look. It was so obvious that he wanted her, more, she suspected, than any man had ever wanted her. She couldn't deny there was more than sexual tension between them. It could be the beginning of a friendship—or something else, something she didn't dare call by name. But whatever it was, it had already been doomed by her lies.

The best thing, the smartest thing, she could do would be to get what she needed and get out. And what she needed was a long talk with him about the night his wife died, not a devastatingly pleasurable afternoon making love.

In time perhaps she would get over her feelings for him, and he might come to understand why she had done what she had done, but not if she followed the dictates of her desires, not if she gave into his erotic charm.

"So, you've thought about it, about us, and what did you decide?" he asked, adjusting the collar of her robe and brushing a damp curl from her face.

"You're my boss," she said.

"Lots of office relationships work out," he countered.

"I don't know you very well," she said, then sheepishly added, "except what I've heard."

He stared at her a moment, then sighed.

She knew exactly what he thought: that she believed the things said about him, that she didn't trust him. And that wasn't true. At this moment, she didn't trust herself. "And you don't know anything about me, except how I feel about you," she said, her heart suddenly painfully full.

"No," he said firmly. "I know what I feel. I've told you—I want you, Landis. I'm the one in the dark here. I don't have any idea what you're feeling."

She lowered her head, staring at her toes beneath her robe, and her voice sounded far away. "I want you, too," she admitted. "But I don't have sex with strangers. Especially strangers I work for."

His hard face softened, but his voice was not apologetic. "Have I pushed too hard?"

"No. But you're lonely, and I'm very confused."

He took her hand and squeezed it, sending a thousand volts of electricity through her.

"I understand," he said, managing another faint smile, then took a deep breath. "Well, then perhaps the best thing *is* to get back to work."

Landis stood on the stone terrace, water dripping from her hair and legs, and watched him slowly disappear into the house.

More than she hated Paula, more than she hated the kind of horrible things that bad television journalism did to people like Ramsey, she hated herself.

~ * ~

Ramsey brought Orphy home from the hospital, and the rest of the week was uneventful. They enjoyed the wonderful food coming from Ivy's fully stocked kitchen, and Landis and Ramsey managed to maintain a normal working relationship.

At least, she thought, it would seem normal to the casual observer. Of course, Ramsey didn't know what was going on in her head or the rest of her when he gave her his reluctant smile or spoke to her in that soft rumbling voice.

And the nights were nearly impossible. Landis heard him at all hours, pacing the house, exercising on his machine, working in the office. She heard him because her own sleep came in broken fragments filled with salacious dreams and dark nightmares.

She had tried distracting herself with her job. But since the job was Ramsey Cain, it proved to be little help. So, she turned her attention back to her snooping and tried to piece together something that would get her out of Kinross House.

The papers she had received from Melba the day of Orphy's accident spelled out Ramsey's professional life and told Orphy's life story as well as Ivy McCreary's. But none of it was unusual, none of it explained how they had all ended up in the thick of a mystery.

She had e-mailed Melba and asked her to dig up all she could on Holly Richards Cain. The unanswered questions all pointed back to Ramsey's late wife, and Landis wanted to understand why.

The information about Holly hadn't been hard to find. Melba faxed the file to Landis within two days. But Landis's bad luck continued, and nothing in the file told her anything she hadn't already learned. It had a brief rundown on Holly's life, her years at Carnegie Mellon

University where she met Ramsey, and her charity work after becoming Mrs. Ramsey Cain; but Landis had gotten more personal information about Holly from her conversation with Orphy.

Vaguely interesting stuff about Holly's older brother, Edward, had led nowhere. The two apparently had a falling out when Holly married Ramsey, and aside from Holly's occasionally giving her brother money to supplement his acting work they had been virtual strangers the last years of her life.

Frustrated, Landis threw the file into her briefcase and picked up the cell phone. If nothing else, maybe Melba could find something on Eberhart. Any clue would be welcome at this point.

"Mel," Landis said, slipping into the bathroom and closing the door.

"Hey, girl," Melba laughed. "How's the spy game?"

"Rotten." Landis took a seat on the toilet. "I've hit a brick wall."

"And is this wall about six-three with long, dark hair?"

"Is everything with you always about sex?" Landis snapped.

"I wasn't talking about sex," her friend shot back. "Do you want to tell me something?"

"No." Landis changed the subject. "Have you discovered anything on Eberhart yet?"

"Yeah," Melba said, and Landis heard the shuffling of papers. "I got an A. Eberhart. She worked for a small theater group out of Boston. She was a costumer—you know, made the stage clothes."

"Holly's brother worked in the theater. Any connection?"

"I can't be certain without a Social Security number to verify everything. Is there any chance you can get it for me?"

Landis laughed. "Oh, sure, the woman loves me. I'll just explain I'm having a little trouble running a background check on her, and I'm sure she'll cooperate."

"I smell sarcasm," Melba said. "Are you having trouble making friends up there?"

Landis sighed. "This one doesn't have friends."

"She might have been friends with Holly's brother," Melba suggested. "Why don't you look up her Social Security number in her personnel file?"

"Good idea, except she was hired through the company, and those files are in Pittsburgh," Landis pointed out.

"Then I guess that leaves only one choice," Melba said with a laugh. "Happy snooping."

"Thanks." Landis shut off the phone and tossed it, along with the files, into her case.

Landis hated to admit it, but Melba was right. If she hoped to find out anything about Eberhart, she'd have to do plenty of snooping.

No time like the present, she decided. She might as well do it while Eberhart was somewhere in the big house earning her living–and before Landis had a chance to talk herself out of it.

She went downstairs first to locate the housekeeper and found her in the library running a vacuum cleaner, with a dust rag and can of polish waiting on the desk.

Hurrying back upstairs, Landis headed for the end of the east wing of the house. She paused a moment to assure herself that she still heard the hum of the vacuum, then hurried up to the third floor. At the top of the stairs a small, dimly-lit hallway, stacked to the rafters with an odd assortment of boxes and trunks, led to the left. To the right was a door set deep in an unpainted wall that looked dingy and forbidding. Landis took a deep breath and turned the knob.

It was locked. The first sign of paranoia was a locked door. And she should know—she'd been locking her door since she got there.

She glanced back down the stairs, then gave the door a hard shake. She leaned down and looked at the antiquated lock. This required a little finesse.

In the far corner a sewing mannequin stood swathed in a graying sheet. She searched through the collection of clutter and found an old sewing kit.

"Pins...not big enough. Ahhh, perfect," she said, pulling a small silver pair of scissors from the box.

The slightly bent tip of the sewing scissors fit easily into the lock. Landis jiggled it and forced it deeper into the mechanism.

"They make this look so easy in the movies," she whispered. "Turn...turn...turn..."

The locked clicked, and the door drifted open with a soft creak.

Landis laughed softly and did her best Sean Connery imitation. "Delaney. Landis Delaney."

Closing the door behind her, she slipped into the housekeeper's bedroom. She was slightly disappointed, and for a moment wondered if she hadn't broken into the wrong room. It was small, too small to be comfortable. A bed, a dresser, a trunk, a small attic window, and a narrow door that probably led to a closet were its only features. There were no rugs or curtains, and the dresser begged for a doily. It looked like a man's room, and one that was strictly temporary, at that.

This is so wrong, she told herself. She was a very bad person for invading the crusty old housekeeper's personal space.

Landis glanced at the dresser standing in the corner, and wondered aloud. "What do you suppose she keeps in there? More ugly gray dresses, some equally ugly underthings... Ahhh, not a pretty thought. You might as well look. Father Palinski says that thinking about it is as bad as doing it."

She crept to the dresser, feeling another wash of guilt, and slid open the top drawer, then stared at the surprising interior.

Empty! So was the second, and the third.

"Well, that doesn't make sense," she complained to the empty room. Eberhart had to have clothes, didn't she? The fourth drawer held a worn pipe and bag of tobacco, and Landis had to bite her lip to keep from laughing. Somehow the mental picture of Eberhart sitting in a room that made an Amish bedroom look inviting, smoking her pipe, was not hard to conjure up.

But the contents of the bottom drawer brought her up short: a few scattered notebooks, a phone book of the Greater Pittsburgh area, and a date book that looked very,

very familiar. Landis plucked the last item from the rest of the clutter.

She opened it. Hundreds of phone numbers filled page after page. Dates and places of meetings going back to August of nineteen ninety-four, all written in Ramsey's familiar strong hand, filled the book.

The infamous missing date book. The same one Ramsey thought was safely tucked in her desk down in the office. She knew that as surely as she knew her own name. But why did Eberhart have it?

Ramsey said that losing the date book had caused numerous problems. And Landis knew those problems were part of the reason he had hired her in the first place. Did Eberhart have something to gain from making Ramsey think his mind was slipping? Was it some sort of demented keepsake, the sort a woman keeps of a man for whom she harbors some hidden affection?

Why was it that, instead of finding answers, all she found were more questions? And who could she ask about it? Certainly not Eberhart. Not Ramsey. Her snooping would only lead to questions she couldn't answer. Orphy? The old woman would likely know what was going on in the house as well as anyone, and she had said that Eberhart was not to be trusted.

Landis stared at the date book. What was she supposed to do with that? Eberhart was obviously a little unhinged—what if she discovered it gone? Maybe somewhere in the soulless room she had a gun, just in case someone or something pushed her over the edge.

Landis hurriedly opened the date book and sprung the rings. She removed the pages and carefully laid the empty cover back in the drawer where she had found it. She tucked the loose pages into her waistband, covered them with her blouse, and hurriedly left the Spartan room, again closing the door behind her. Slipping quietly down the stairs, she hurried to her room and secreted the contents of the date book in her suitcase with the cell phone.

She was certain now; it wasn't her imagination. Something was definitely going on at Kinross House, something more than a not-so-missing date book and secretive housekeepers. If the police photos hadn't been included in the file on Ramsey she had studied before coming to Kinross House, Landis might have believed Eberhart was keeping a deranged Holly captive in the attic.

Landis paused and, casting a glance at the high, ornate ceiling of her bedroom, listened for a moment. "This is nuts," she muttered to herself and, opening the door to the empty office, got back to work on the computer files.

~ * ~

Ramsey felt like a caged tiger. He waited until he heard Landis call it a night, then escaped the confines of his bedroom to pace the library.

Being so close to her and not being able to touch her was pure torture. And the little scene at the pool had only made things worse. He wanted to touch her silken skin, to kiss her mouth, to make her sigh...

Why did he do this to himself? he wondered. He'd had more than his share of women. Before his marriage he'd had no problem with the female of the species. One of his fraternity brothers had laughingly said that somewhere in Pittsburgh there was a mill where they made nothing but beautiful women for Ramsey. His social life had been fine. No, better than fine.

And even after Holly's death there had been certain females who sought him out, the sort who found the idea of being with a man accused of murder the ultimate turn-on. Of course, he'd had no interest in them.

It reminded him of an old joke. *I wouldn't be caught dead with the sort of woman who would date me.*

It was as though he had to put that part of himself away, as though his body grew as numb as his heart.

So, his social life had ground to a halt, and, frankly, he hadn't missed it. Until Landis!

Suddenly, he could feel again. And his body was apparently hell-bent to make up for lost time. When she was near he felt as though he were a single giant nerve, hot and prickly and sensitive to the slightest change in the air. His body reacted to everything. Her nearness, her smile, her laugh... Hell, even sitting down at the drafting table brought back memories that made him hard and edgy.

Ramsey opened the French doors leading to the patio. A storm brewed. Weather reports mentioned a front moving in from the northwest. It would take its own sweet time crossing into the foothills, and the change in barometric pressure would affect everyone.

~ * ~

Edward turned on the light over the mirror. He had chosen his costume carefully. The right attire could make or break a performance, and this would be the scene of his lifetime.

He laughed. "Title it *The Death of The Substitute*."

154

He knew Cain was still awake—knew, too, that this was the perfect time for a dress rehearsal. He adjusted the black-ribbed material higher on his neck and carefully slipped on the black ski mask and gloves. Then, just as cautiously, he turned off the light.

~ * ~

Ramsey emptied his glass and stopped to listen to the sounds of traffic on the highway. He really should stop drinking. He set the empty decanter on the patio table. But good old Eberhart kept the house too generously supplied, and he hadn't cared much about sobriety lately.

It was ironic that, even though he had been a drinker at college and socially after that, all the time Holly had been downing the booze he had not touched the stuff. After her death, which the world blamed on him and he blamed on Gordon's London Dry Gin, he had turned to the bottle himself, perhaps finishing himself slowly the way Holly had. Wouldn't a shrink have a field day with that one!

One thing was certain, he thought, turning to the house. Drinking made him morbid and it certainly didn't help stop his thoughts of Landis Delaney.

He locked the French doors, passed through the library, and headed up the staircase. For a second he thought he sensed something at the top of the stairs, but it must have been the shifting light. He told himself it was time to change the fixture, that a brighter light, perhaps an ornate chandelier, would illuminate that space better. But not tonight. Tonight the dim light suited him.

~ * ~

Edward pressed himself into the shadows and waited as Cain slowly climbed the stairs with deliberate steps, putting one foot carefully in front of the other the way a man did when he knew he'd had too much to drink. When his enemy was still a few feet away Edward smelled the whiskey.

It would be so easy. All he had to do was reach out of the darkness and send the man plummeting down the dark stairs. It would be fitting; it would be poetic. Edward's hand fairly itched to do it.

But then it would be over. Cain's pain and suffering would stop, and his debt would be canceled.

Edward held his hand in check, held his breath so as not to disturb the air around them. A battle raged inside him unlike any he'd ever known before. This was just a dress rehearsal, he reminded himself, not the performance he wanted—the performance he needed. The plan was to kill Landis and to make Ramsey suffer, not end his suffering once and for all.

Edward held himself perfectly still as Cain walked past.

He waited until Cain had closed the door to the office before he stepped again from the shadows. He sweated, but it felt good. The hatred, the fury, the lust for blood flooded his veins, pumping with his blood into every cell of his body.

"Soon," he whispered through the damp ski mask. "Very soon."

Ten

Sunday morning dawned hot and oppressive. The valley shimmered in hazy summer light. It wasn't normal for western Pennsylvania to experience so many days of sunshine in a row. Now, apparently, it would more than make up for it. A storm brewed in the west, and from the persistent rumble of thunder in the distance it promised to be a doozy.

Landis wore a simple summer dress that kept her reasonably cool. She stood on the patio off the library and watched clouds boil in the distance. The tops of the dark spires rose into the deep blue of the summer sky, an ominous portent of things to come.

"It looks as though the weather might get nasty." Ramsey's voice, so close behind her, made her jump.

"I didn't hear you come out," she said, stating the obvious.

"You were intent on watching the gathering storm." He stepped next to her and turned his attention to the sky above the valley. "Ivy and Eberhart both have the night off, and since Aunt Orphy is a hundred-and-ten percent again, she's spending the evening in Kittanning with friends. This might be a good opportunity for you to visit friends or family yourself."

"My family lives on the other side of the county. I couldn't get there before the storm hit. I don't mind staying here alone with you." She watched his profile for some reaction. None was forthcoming.

"You romantic types rather like this sort of thing, don't you?" Ramsey's voice was thoughtful as he continued to watch the lowering sky.

Landis couldn't decide if he teased her or not.

He added, "Dark mansions on stormy nights and a troubled soul to nurse."

"First of all, I told you before I am *not* a romantic." She wasn't sure why his words piqued her. Perhaps it was because she didn't want to admit how true they might be. The old cool-and-analytical Landis wasn't a romantic. This new Landis seemed to have a deplorable romantic streak and, at that very moment, experienced an erotic jolt from just standing close to this enigmatic figure in his gothic surroundings. "Second," she pointed out, "there are plenty of lights in this house."

Her voice might have sounded cool, but she had the strongest urge to touch him, to just reach out and run her hand over his shoulder. To compensate for her disturbing desires and for feeling on the defensive, Landis did the worst possible thing. She went on the attack. "And, third, I don't think you're all that troubled."

"Really?" he said, raising an elegant brow at her assessment of him. "I don't think you could possibly comprehend the depth of my trouble."

"It sounds more like self-pity."

He turned to her, his face a dark mask of interest and perhaps a touch of annoyance. "What does that mean?"

"I mean, you shut yourself away in this house, nursing your own troubled soul, *thank you very much*, and blaming the world for how unfairly it treated you. Instead of going out and proving it wrong. I think you're the one with romantic notions about yourself. You see yourself as this dark, paradoxical Beast—"

"Paradoxical? Beast?"

"—spurned by life, and waiting for a...a fair maiden to rescue you. I can tell you this Ramsey Cain. You're going to be disappointed. Life doesn't work like a Disney film. The Beast has to work on himself and the maiden has troubles of her own."

~ * ~

Ramsey stood in stunned silence as she turned on her heels and headed back into the house. For a long time after she left him alone on the terrace, he thought about what she'd said. At first he thought she was crazy; he wasn't feeling sorry for himself. By the time the rain had begun to fall in fat drops on the flagstones, he thought perhaps there could be a grain of truth to her words, as much as it pained him to admit it.

There were things he could change. He had come to the country because of Holly, and now, in a twisted sort of way, he stayed because of her. Perhaps closing up the house and moving back to the city would be best for all of them. Leave his past and his ghosts there to torment themselves.

He could find a nice apartment. Better yet, he could rent something and build a new place in Upper St. Clair or

Fox Chapel, something bright and airy that would more suit a woman like Landis than this dark, antiquated mansion.

He glanced at the French doors to see if she had come back for round two–and was disappointed to not find her there.

In the days that followed their encounter in the office, Ramsey had done little but work, worry about Orphy, and think about Landis. He had come to the understanding that, though he knew little about her, she had grown to be very important to him. He had feelings for her, real feelings that could not be ignored.

However, he also knew if he pushed her she would pull away. The troubles she had hinted at during her angry dressing-down were real and lurking just beneath the surface. He had seen them in her rejection of him and in the nightmares that made her every bit as restless as his made him.

He had waited to confront her with what was happening between them. Now, he was certain the wait would soon come to an end.

~ * ~

Landis's hand shook as she closed her bedroom door. She wasn't sure if anger or fear made her tremble. She wasn't sure what she felt. She had lashed out at Ramsey because there had been so much truth in everything she said.

She did see him in an unrealistic light and she did see a troubled soul. She had never been so confused by any man. When she walked into his library that first day, she'd had a clear picture of Ramsey Cain, of a man who had killed his wife and gotten away with it.

Now that she knew him better, that picture seemed out of place. Certainly, the man who had taken her in his arms, who had kissed her with such hunger and need, was a man driven by passion, but not the passion to kill.

It wasn't right. He was dark, mysterious, harder to understand than any man she had ever known, but she no longer believed he was capable of murdering his wife. And that thought scared the hell out of her. If he was innocent, she was party to an act more reprehensible than she had originally believed. And she was in danger not of losing her life but of losing her heart.

The idea that she might be falling in love with this man frightened her beyond words. She had to do something. She thought about calling Paula. Over the last couple of days, quitting her job had become a recurring fantasy. If she quit, she could tell Ramsey everything. And she would find work somewhere. If she were really lucky she might find a television station that understood her insubordination. And if no station would hire her, a researcher with her qualifications could find work at a university or a newspaper. If she walked away now, maybe Ramsey would understand, maybe he could even forgive her in time.

She knew none of that would happen. It had gone too far already. Still, she had to find some way out. She sat, staring at the cell phone, when another of the sore spots on her guilty conscience began to gnaw at her.

Her parents.

She had told them she would be away on business for a couple of weeks, but she had promised to call them and she hadn't. Now she wished Ramsey hadn't mentioned visiting her family. It only reminded her of her thoughtlessness.

She picked up the phone and dialed the number. The answering machine picked up, and the familiar sound of her mother's voice reassured her.

"Hi, Mom. It's me," she said after the beep. "I just wanted to check in and tell you everything's fine. I should be finished with this job soon. I'll stop in and visit. Give Dad a hug for me. Love you."

She turned off the phone and gave a sigh of relief. If only fixing her conscience were so easy where Ramsey was concerned.

~ * ~

The storm hit the house with all the force Mother Nature could rally. The windows shook, and the rain sounded like rocks striking the glass. Thunder rumbled through and around the valley, echoing back on itself. It was what Landis's grandmother called a "gully washer."

By that evening, the lights that Landis had insisted separated her from one of Emily Bronte's heroines were out. From the window Cherry Run was dark and indistinguishable from the woods that lay beyond, lit only by intermittent flashes of blue-white light.

She felt the static electricity along her arms and at her nape. It was the storm, she told herself, but she wondered if it might not be that she was alone in the house with Ramsey. She opened her bedroom door and found he had lit a hurricane lamp at the top of the stairs. She checked the office and found it empty. Taking a deep breath, she knocked on his door but got no answer. Finally, she went downstairs.

Landis found him in the kitchen, looking in the refrigerator with a flashlight. "The food will stay colder if the door stays closed."

He looked up. "Mrs. McCreary left us a lovely lasagna, but I'm afraid tonight it's a cold dinner."

Landis wrinkled her nose. Cold lasagna sounded positively awful. "Let me get a look," she said, pushing in next to him.

Ramsey handed her the flashlight. "Help yourself, and if you find something, give a whistle."

"Where are you going?" She let the beam of light hit him in the face for a split second.

"I won't be far," he said, shielding his eyes.

A quick check of the refrigerator told Landis that Ivy did most of her cooking from scratch. There were plenty of ingredients but nothing she could make in a hurry without a stove.

She removed bologna and cheese, mayonnaise, and mustard. She found pickles and lettuce for the finishing touch. It took her no time at all to make up a plate of sandwiches. It didn't show off her culinary ability at its best, but at least they'd have something to eat.

She balanced the plates. With her hip, she pushed open the door to the dining room, then stopped in her tracks.

The room was ablaze with soft candlelight. Almost every surface held at least a handful of glittering tapers. They flickered in the breeze of the swinging door, sparkled with warmth, and reflected in the mirrors over the mantelpiece and the buffet.

She smiled at Ramsey who poured wine into crystal glasses.

"Good timing," he said softly. His voice sent a jolt of anxious energy through Landis.

"I'm afraid you're going to be disappointed," she said with a sigh. "All I came up with were bologna sandwiches."

His answering smile made her feel warm all over. He looked at the bottle of wine, and his smile broadened. "Perfect. Just what I'd serve with bologna. We'll make it a picnic."

He slipped off his shoes and stepped up on one of the chairs, then sat on the table top.

"You'll ruin the table," she warned, but Ramsey had already seated himself cross-legged in the center. She set the plates down and let him take her hand to help her up. She spread her skirt and sat down across from him.

He lifted his glass. "To dark and stormy nights." He touched his glass to hers.

She sipped the warm wine, and her cheeks flamed at the memory of what she had said to him on the patio. "I'm sorry I said those things to you earlier," she said sheepishly. "You've had more than your share of trouble, and I had no right to criticize you."

"No," he said, putting down his glass and taking her hand. "You held up a mirror to me, Landis, and I didn't like what I saw. Some of those troubles...some of them were out of my control, but others came about from my own bad choices. I chose to stay in this house, and I chose to isolate myself. It was a mistake, and I need to do something about that."

He kissed her hand, and the heat in her veins increased to a simmer. "I thank you for those observations." He released her and looked at the plate of sandwiches. "I'm starved."

They ate and talked about the most mundane things: the mall, the difference in garlic and kosher bologna, and why electricity was more susceptible to failures in small towns than in the city. Landis felt comfortable and happy with the conversation. She felt at home, in sync with him. Before she realized it, she found herself answering questions about her past.

"I was born in Kittanning Township," she told him.

"Really? That's not far from here," he said, genuinely surprised.

She had to remind herself that he didn't have stacks of information on her the way she did about him. He only knew what she'd written on the fictionalized resume.

"I thought your parents lived on the other side of the county," he said, and a red warning flag danced in Landis's brain.

"They moved to Ford City after I moved out," she lied. Her parents would have no more left the house they built in the early sixties than they would have sprouted wings. They were country people, through and through.

"Do you have brothers and sisters?" he asked.

"Two sisters, Valerie and Kimberly. Val's married with kids, and Kimmy works for a doctor in Leechburg."

"It must have been great having sisters," he said, and Landis thought she heard a touch of wistfulness in his voice. He must have wanted siblings; and she could almost see him, a grubby ten-year-old wrestling in the grass with a handful of equally grubby brothers.

"Oh, yeah, sisters are great, if you don't mind sharing a room and clothes and friends and a bathroom and—"

"You're making me glad I was an only child," he said.

"We weren't your typical family," she replied, analyzing her childhood. "Mom is very independent, and she raised us to be three individuals instead of treating us as a group. She would always refer to us separately. We were Valerie, Kimberly and Landis. Never 'the girls.' So we grew up not to need each other. I don't talk to my sisters very much."

"That's too bad," he said.

Landis suddenly felt very vulnerable because of what she'd said. She hadn't meant to tell so much.

"I always wondered what it would be like to have a close family." He drank deeply from his wine glass.

"You and Orphy seem very close," she observed.

"Yes, but it isn't the same as having brothers and sisters. But we're not talking about me. So, you have sisters and parents and—what...a dog?"

"Cat," Landis said, smiling at the memory. "Her name is Jelly Jar, and she's the oldest, fattest cat in three counties."

"Jelly Jar?"

"When we got her, dad said she was small enough to fit in a jelly jar, and it sort of stuck. We just call her Jell. My father hated that cat—or said he did. Now that he's retired Jelly follows him around, and he watches football with her on his lap."

"What did your father do?"

"He was a coal miner, what else?" She noticed a questioning look in Ramsey's eyes. She knew what he was wondering. "Yes, he mined for Bitter Clay, and so did my grandpa."

"So, your family was very fond of mine, I take it?" He grinned knowingly.

"Oh, yeah, Dad had a list of pet names for your grandfather."

Ramsey laughed. "I bet he did. My father hated mining. Said no one should have to go down in those holes for a living. But he was sorry he sold out after he saw how the mines declined."

"It was probably for the best, " Landis said. "If he had tried to save the mines the way you're trying to save Cain-Dunham your family would have been broke years ago. I think what you did was wonderful. Most businessmen would have bailed out and left the company to fold. Saving it was...honorable."

"'Honorable' is not a word most people would use to describe me." He took her hand and kissed it. "It's my company; saving it wasn't honorable. I created the problem. The people who worked for me didn't deserve to pay for what happened after Holly's death."

A strange light came into his eyes, and Landis knew the time had come to ask. "Can you talk about that night?" she asked softly. "Orphy said Holly was a difficult woman, that she lied to you to get you to marry her and that she drank."

He listened to her as she told him everything she and his aunt had discussed, and his face grew dark. "She did fill you in, didn't she?"

"I'm sorry," Landis said quickly. "I didn't mean to pry."

"Holly was a beautiful woman. She had a lot of admirers. Why she wanted me was a mystery."

Landis knew why, but she said nothing.

"She used to laugh and say she chased me 'till I caught her, but there was some truth in that. A lot of people tried to warn me: Bridget, Orphy, some of my fraternity brothers. But I didn't listen. I thought she was as sweet on the inside as she looked on the outside. Stupid to assume such a thing, but I did."

He drained his wine glass, then refilled it, inclining the bottle to Landis, who shook her head.

"She told me she thought she was pregnant. I guess I wanted to believe her. We were married here in the garden. Later, the doctor said it was a false alarm because her tests kept coming back negative. Again, I was stupid to assume she wasn't just lying. But I had been brought up to tell the truth."

Landis's heart pinched. She'd lied to him, too. Maybe she was no better than Holly. Except...she looked into his haunted dark eyes and saw much more than a wealthy man she could dupe. Landis saw a man she could have loved, if fate hadn't had such a twisted sense of humor.

"Holly and I managed to live together for almost eight years. She had her interests, and I had the business, and we had enough feelings for each other to make it passable. Until I wanted to start a family. Holly didn't want children.

She said they would be a burden and would interfere with her life. It created a strain in an already weak marriage. I grew distant, inattentive, and she found a hell of a way to get back at me."

He ran a hand through his hair, sighed. "She picked one of the most obnoxious, bragging asses I knew, and she slept with him. Within the week everyone in our circle of friends was talking. Actually, they were laughing—at me."

"But she was the one who cheated," Landis protested indignantly.

Ramsey gave her a sympathetic look. "Among my circle of friends it's not the act of betrayal that counts, it's who was stupid enough to get hurt."

"Some friends," Landis said sharply.

"Well, I showed her," he said, his voice taking on an awful passion. "I sold that mausoleum of a house and packed her off to the country. I took away everything that mattered to her. I told her if she so much as set foot off this estate I'd divorce her and hire one of those high-profile divorce lawyers to hide my assets so she'd get nothing. I had the last laugh."

The passion drained out of his voice. "The last laugh," he repeated. "That's a good one. Things were so much worse. I'd come home and find her drinking, or sobbing, or cursing me. I told her she could go back anytime she wanted but reminded her that she'd end up with nothing. I wanted to punish her for what she had done to me."

Landis saw pain in his face, and her heart ached with it. "She wanted a settlement?" she asked, her shaky voice little more than a whisper.

"And in lieu of that she would settle for driving me nuts. But she was the one who was isolated; she was the one who came from a background of instability."

He stopped and drank deeply from his glass. "The night she died she'd been drinking for three straight days. She ran out of scotch and had gone to the library for a bottle of old whiskey I kept in the drawer. We met at the top of the stairs. I told her to give me the bottle, and we argued. I called her a drunk, told her she was just like her mother. She tried to slap me, and her nails grazed my neck."

His fingers brushed the scars on his neck. "I caught her hand and flung it away. She became wild, threw herself at me, screaming and cursing. All I did was put up my hands. I wanted to stop her. She stumbled on the edge of the landing...The next thing I knew, she was dead."

Landis let loose the breath she had been holding. The story was the same one he had told at the inquest. She understood now why the coroner and the district attorney's office had not pressed charges. She knew, just as they must have, that every word he said was true. There was too much pain, too much guilt in Ramsey's eyes for it to have happened any other way.

She believed him, and her heart broke for him.

"So, you see," he said finally. "I didn't murder my wife, but if I had just let her go, just given her what she wanted, she would be alive now."

"You can't hold yourself responsible for her death," Landis insisted. "It was an accident."

"I could have done things differently. The rumors, the gossip, that damn woman reporter who hounded me for months—I deserved it all, but the people at Cain-Dunham didn't deserve it. It isn't nobility that makes me fight to save the company. I just need to save some small part of my own soul."

"I think anyone who can survive what you have is noble."

Ramsey got off the table and, taking her by the waist, pulled her with him. "I am not noble," he said in a voice filled with anger.

He kissed her, searing her mouth with his own, pushing past her surprised resistance as if to prove to her his motives weren't honorable. Landis's response was to give, to part her lips willingly and answer his demands with needs of her own. She slid her arms around his neck and pressed her body to his, until he tore his mouth from hers with a groan.

The kiss left her breathless.

He brushed his mouth over the curve of her jaw and breathed a soft curse. "I promised you I wouldn't do this again," he said in a strained whisper. "But I want you so..."

He released her. Landis felt the loss immediately and watched as he lifted a single candlestick and, turning, left the dining room, leaving her alone with her own desire.

Eleven

Landis blew out all the candles Ramsey had left in the dinning room with the exception of one in a lovely old silver candlestick. She took it, along with the dirty dishes, into the kitchen. As the door closed behind her, the tears came. She put the dishes in the sink, the candle on the work table, and gripped the edge of the counter as wave after wave of sobs racked her body.

She had never known such sorrow, never felt someone else's pain so keenly. It broke her heart, remembering the expression on his face as he told his story. She had wanted nothing more than to ease that pain, to erase the lines of sorrow that had left their mark on his handsome face.

When the storm inside Landis had passed, she felt drained but more determined than ever. The truth stared her in the face, daring her to do the right thing. And until this moment she hadn't known what that was. Now she knew.

Rationally, Landis understood that following her troubled heart might be a mistake, but she had stopped being rational; and since she'd met Ramsey Cain she had already made lots of mistakes. It had been a mistake to think she could come into Ramsey's house, into his life, and then leave with her heart unscathed.

She would leave—she knew that now—but too much had happened for her to walk away without some kind of resolution. She had to find a way to fix the trouble she had caused. Quitting her job would be a good start, but there was so much more to do. Ramsey said he didn't know how she felt about him. Tonight, she would show him.

She crossed the dining room and went into the foyer. The candle in her hand threw wild shadows as she went up the stairs, and, as always, her thoughts turned to Holly.

How ironic, she thought. That she would want so desperately all the things Holly had thrown away: the quiet of this small town, the peace of life away from the stressful pace of the city, and Ramsey. How had Holly lived with him and not seen what a treasure she had? Or had none of that been important to her?

Well, it meant the world to Landis.

A shadow fell over her from the oil light at the top of the stairs, and Landis glanced up expecting to see Ramsey looking down at her. She said his name softly and suddenly knew that this silent form watching her wasn't Ramsey. It was tall, but too thin. Could it be just a trick of the light? She thought it was a man, but...

"Eberhart, is that you?"

Again the shadow did not answer or move, and a sense of panic washed over her. There was a stranger in the house. Was it a burglar? Where was Ramsey? She thought of her cut brake line, and her breath knotted in her throat.

A flash of lightning bathed the dark foyer. Landis thought she caught a glimpse of a figure dressed in black from head to foot, its features obscured by a raised hand.

"Who are you?" she shouted.

Somewhere in the great house a door opened and closed with a bang. But the foyer had gone dark again, and now Landis wasn't sure she had seen anything. The light at the top of the stairs shifted and wavered as Ramsey came into view. The candle he carried added its feeble light to that of the lamp. Landis could clearly see the empty landing.

~ * ~

"Did you call out?" Ramsey asked, his tone rich with concern.

"Where did he go?" she asked, hurrying to join him on the landing.

"Who?" Ramsey lifted the candle and looked into the foyer. Something had frightened Landis, and he was half-afraid of who, or *what*, might be standing at the foot of the stairs.

"I saw someone." She shivered so violently that Ramsey reached for her. He pulled her to his side and again looked out over the railing.

"Not down there." She pulled him back. "Up here."

He looked at her, all wide-eyed and trembling. Something had really scared her. Ramsey pulled her close and held her for a moment. "It was probably my shadow from down the hall."

"No!" she insisted. "I saw someone, and he—"

"It was a man?"

"I don't know," she cried, frustrated. "I thought it was."

"Where did he go?"

"He...just...vanished."

"I'll go look around. You wait in the office."

"No!" she said, burrowing closer. "I'm going with you."

He liked the way she clung to his side. He liked the way she looked up at him as though she felt safe beside him. But he knew who, or what, had scared her. He didn't need to look anywhere. It had to have been the specter of his late wife.

"Come on," he said, keeping a protective arm around her. "I think all you need is a good stiff drink."

"I've had enough wine," she said, her wide eyes gazing up into his. "Maybe that's all it was. I'm not used to expensive wines, and it made me see things."

"Did you have enough to conjure up a first-class boogie man?" he asked, leading her down the hall to the west wing. He walked past her bedroom door and led her into the office.

"I have an equally expensive bottle of whiskey in my room," he suggested. "Maybe we should see what that would do to you."

~ * ~

"I feel a lot better," Landis said. Maybe the shadow *had* been just a figment of her imagination, and the wine, and the dark and stormy night, and the intense emotions that churned inside her. "I think I'll just get ready for bed."

Ramsey smiled at her, but Landis thought she saw disappointment on his face as she opened the door to her room. But she couldn't take his unmistakable invitation...not just yet.

Her heart beat like a triphammer as she showered and blew her hair dry. She dressed in her short satin nightgown and slipped into her robe. Before she left the bathroom she reached into her bag for the cell phone. She let the events of the last few days fuel the angry fire that had ignited in her when Ramsey told her the truth about his life. Like molten lava in her stomach, the frustration and the pain of the last few weeks fused together until the voice at the other end of the phone prompted an eruption.

"It's me," Landis said, her voice strained with the rage that boiled inside her. "I have one thing to say, so shut-up and listen."

"I beg your—"

"I quit."

There was a long pause, and Landis heard Paula sputter. "What did you say?"

"You're an egotistical bully. You think your position gives you the power to ruin peoples' lives. Well, you're not going to ruin mine, and if I can stop you, you're not going to ruin Ramsey's."

"'Ramsey,' is it," Paula said with derision. "I should have guessed. You've fallen in love with that maniac. Or have you just fallen into his bed? Well, listen to me, you stupid—"

"I don't have to take any more of your garbage—and one last thing. I'm going to the station manager. I'll tell him about the doctored release forms. I'll go to every single person whose words you've scrambled for the last year and volunteer to testify against you. I'll sue the station myself for unethical practices. There is an old saying, Paula. Payback's a bitch."

Landis slammed the little phone shut, and all the anger and the frustration escaped her body in one deep breath. She stared at her reflection in the foggy mirror for a second, her heart beating erratically in her chest and her breath painful in her breast; but she felt like a weight had been lifted off her.

Slowly, she put a dab of perfume at her wrists and in her cleavage, then, focusing on her plan, remembered one last thing. Opening her purse, she began to root through the collective junk. They had to be in here somewhere. Melba had given her a box as a joke last Christmas. She had carried them around with her ever since. Now, damn it, she couldn't find them.

She found them wedged between a folder of computer disks and an old box of Junior Mints. An unopened box of condoms. She took a foil-wrapped packet out of the box and slipped it into her pocket, then, thinking better of it, took a second. With a deep breath, Landis opened the door and slipped into the office.

She stood for a moment outside his bedroom, the cool doorknob in her hand. She was nervous. She had only known a couple of men intimately, and the last had been so long ago she had begun to think the statute of limitations had surely run out on her sexuality. Certainly, neither of her past lovers had been anything like Ramsey. They had been safe and predictable. Ramsey was anything but predictable.

Suddenly, the nickname Bridget had laughed about popped into her head, and her stomach did a nervous little flip-flop. Ramrod. A thousand nasty little possibilities flashed through Landis's head.

"Oh, for heaven sakes. Just do it," she chided herself in a whisper and pushed the door open.

He stood at the Palladian window that dominated one wall, his back to her, holding a drink in his hand. He turned, surprised to see her. He looked disheveled and sexy with his shirt unbuttoned and pulled free from his slacks. The candle he had left on the dresser cast him in a warm light, caressing the hard planes of his face and sharp contours of his chest.

He took her breath away. For a long moment she couldn't say anything. She let her gaze follow the open shirt up from his flat stomach to the strong surface of his chest to his incredibly handsome face.

"I decided I needed that drink," she lied. What she needed stood at the window watching her with dark and longing eyes.

He reached for the bottle on the table next to him and poured a second glass of rich amber liquid. "I didn't think you—"

"Your trouble is you think too much," she said with a smile. The soft carpet beneath her bare feet made her tread silent as she crossed the room to join him at the window. She watched him watching her, and her heart filled to overflowing.

A flash of lightning cast light on the front yard and the old gate that had squeaked when she'd opened it that first day.

"You watched me come up that sidewalk, didn't you?" she asked, looking up at him.

"Yes, and I knew you were going to be trouble."

She smiled and sipped her whiskey. It burned away her hesitation, and her nerves. She wanted this closeness as much as she wanted all the rest. "I felt your gaze on me then, but I didn't think you were going to be trouble at all. Of course, when I came here I believed a lot of things that weren't true."

"You believed I killed my wife," he said, and she heard the pain in his voice.

"I believed what I'd heard."

He stepped closer, taking the glass of whiskey from her hand and placed it with his own on the table.

"And now?" he asked, watching her with those unreadable eyes, and she knew in that instant that she loved him, that she had loved him for a long time, and that no matter what happened tomorrow or the day after she would love him always.

It began as a gentle caress. Landis touched the smooth, dark skin beneath his open shirt. She slid her hands up to his collar and wound her arms around his neck.

"Now, I believe in you," she whispered.

He said nothing, but pulled her to him and covered her mouth with his.

His kiss touched her deeply, reaching into her soul, and Landis gave it back—and more. She wanted to feel him to the core of her being, marking her as his own. She wanted the kiss to last forever.

The last time she had been in his arms he had led her. This time she wanted to lead him. She wanted to show him the way to her heart, to the passion they would share. So she stepped away from him, sure in the knowledge that he would see her in the erratic lightning and the soft candlelight. She slid her hand into her pocket, securing her little treasures, then opened her robe and dropped it to the floor. She slid her hands down her nightgown and watched his gaze follow. Catching the edge of her hem, she lifted the gown over her head, letting it fall to the floor with her robe.

Ramsey drew a ragged breath, looking at her, but did not touch her. His gaze moved over her, over the lines and curves of a body Landis had always thought lacked anything special.

His face told her something else. In his eyes she was perfect. He made her feel beautiful. It made her want him more keenly than she had thought possible.

Holding the condoms between her fingers, she reached out and opened the snap at his waistband. He closed his eyes briefly, as though it caused him pain, but he did nothing to stop her. She could see his desire come to life as she slid his trousers down his thickly muscled legs.

Kneeling in front of him to retrieve his pants, she heard him moan but didn't have a chance to do anything more. He reached down and pulled her up to meet him. In a moment she was in his arms, and together they landed with a bounce on the satin-covered bed.

~ * ~

Ramsey was certain he couldn't stand it another moment. He needed to touch her, to feel her beneath him, around him. But she seemed intent on driving him mad.

She slid to the side and pressed him back onto the bed. She didn't say a word, but her intent was clear. He

180

thought if she touched him he might explode. But her touch was soft, precise and purposeful, and he gave himself over to it.

Landis kissed him deeply, drawing away his breath. She trailed kisses down the scars on his neck and over his shoulder. She ran her tongue over his pectoral until he thought he was on fire, then caught a hard nipple in her strong, white teeth.

He groaned and dropped his head back on the pillow. He had never felt this before, this utter loss of control. He reveled in her kisses and the hot feel of her mouth as she slid down his body. When she took him into her mouth, Ramsey was certain that he would die. He was certain that his heart would fragment into a million aching pieces.

The act itself was generous. And while he had experienced it before he had never felt this profound sense of closeness. He wanted to give himself over to it, but it wasn't enough. He had to feel her, all of her. He wanted her release. He wanted to give her as much as she had given him.

Landis was lost in the joy of her task when she felt his fingers dig into her arms and pull her away. She smiled at him.

"You are a wicked woman," he said against her mouth.

"You have no idea." Landis laughed as she righted herself, and tore open one of the foil packs with her teeth. The latex was warm from her hand, and she took her time unrolling it over him. She laughed again at his expression as she straddled his body and lowered herself onto him, and with one hard thrust he filled her, turning the laugh into a gasp of pleasure.

He stopped and waited for her to say or do something. Landis rocked her hips forward, pushing him deeper into her body.

Then it all became a blur, a frenzy of feelings and erotic whispers that pushed Landis deeper and deeper into a fog of sensations she had never known before. And always there was Ramsey, his mouth, his hands, his body to lead her, to edge her closer until she thought she would come apart in his hands.

He sat up, shifting inside her, and every movement brought another response from her body. In a sudden explosion of exotic passion, Landis pulled herself to him so she wouldn't lose him in that fog and screamed his name. She felt him shudder inside her, and together they fell back onto the bed, clinging to each other.

For a long moment, Landis lay curled in his arms. They didn't say a word. Whether it was because neither wanted to break the spell nor because they had no breath left to talk Landis wasn't sure, but she loved that moment. Filled with contentment, she wanted to lie there and feel his arms around her a little longer, so she was surprised when she heard her own voice.

"Ramsey," she whispered.

His answer was a soft hum in her ear.

"I..." she hesitated, and Ramsey pulled her closer, kissing her neck.

"You...?" he prompted

"I think I'm falling in love with you," she said softly.

His kisses stopped, and he tensed. "Are you sure that's wise?"

She turned in his arms, taking his face into her hands. "I don't care if it isn't wise. I don't care about the past or the future. And I don't care if loving you is right or wrong."

~ * ~

Ramsey watched her silently. He wanted to tell her, to see her face when he whispered words of love in return. But it had been so long he didn't think he had the words to convey how he felt. He kissed her again and felt a fresh rush of passion.

"You taste like sunshine," he said softly. "You feel like satin, warmed with a touch. I have never known a woman like you, Landis Delaney."

He kissed her slowly, pressing her back onto the bed. "You make me feel alive again," he said, stretching her arms over her head. The movement made her perfect breasts sway seductively, and he took the opportunity presented. Holding her hands firmly, he lowered his mouth to one taut nipple. He lavished attention on her, first one breast and then the other, until Landis moaned and wiggled beneath him.

"I want you to know what I feel," he said against the soft skin of her belly.

Landis writhed as he released her hands and took his time trailing kisses down her body. She had his assurance that loving him wasn't a mistake. He intended to love her so thoroughly that there would be no room for doubts.

As he reached the dewy curls at the apex of her thighs, Landis sighed and wound her fingers into his hair.

Ramsey kissed her, urged on by her small groans of pleasure to deepen the kiss.

She did taste like sunshine, and he lost himself in her until he heard her call his name and felt her shuddered release. Only then did he give into his own powerful desire and kiss his way back to her waiting mouth. He slipped into her welcoming body and found at last a haven for his wounded soul.

~ * ~

Edward listened to the sounds coming from Ramsey's room with barely contained disgust, then turned off the intercom. He wished he could have stopped them.

"How dare they foul this place?" he growled to the reflection in the mirror. "How dare he defile Holly's memory with his lust for that woman? I should slip down there now and slit their throats in their sleep. I should kill them both. It would serve them right. But it would ruin my carefully laid plan. And Ramsey Cain has ruined enough in my life. He won't ruin my moment of glory, and he won't ruin Holly's chance to have her vengeance."

He turned the intercom back on and listened, but all he heard was the soft rustle of the bed and the sounds of blissful sleep. He thought about what he'd heard. What they had said and what they had done, and his stomach lurched. He waited for the roiling to stop, but the images in his head had begun to change. It was no longer Ramsey and Landis he saw in his mind's eye.

It was a woman, her eyes glittering with desire and her mouth hungrily rooting at a strange man's lips. She opened her blouse, and her breasts bobbed until the man began to touch them. In the doorway, ten-year-old Eddie Richards wanted to look away. He wanted to go back to his safe, quiet bed, but he couldn't move.

His mother fiddled with the man's pants. Their laughter floated on the smoke-filled air. After a moment she climbed off his lap and onto her knees in front of the stranger's chair. Eddy's eyes grew wide as he watched, and a scream lodged in his throat, strangling him.

In the quiet attic room, Edward closed his eyes and tears rolled down his cheeks, but the rumble in his stomach continued until he finally reached for the basin and emptied his belly. When it was past Edward wiped his mouth and crawled into his bed. He hated them all: his slut of a mother; all those strange men who brought her booze and wriggled under her skirt for payment; and Ramsey Cain, who had killed the only person he had ever truly loved.

Twelve

Landis opened her eyes and found Ramsey smiling at her.

"Good morning...again," he said, kissing her shoulder.

"Good morning," she sighed. She couldn't remember a time when she felt so wonderful...or so scared.

Ramsey rolled out of the bed and crossed to the dresser that stood at the far wall. Landis watched him walk away and marveled. He was so painfully beautiful. Every inch of him was perfect, each step he took was filled with grace and strength. The muscles of his back bunched and flexed as he took a pair of boxer shorts out of the drawer and twirled them on one finger.

Never in her wildest fantasy had Landis seen herself in the arms of such a man. She never thought she would find herself watching the personification of everything that was incredible about the male of the species casually walk around the room gathering his clothes.

She gave him a wolf whistle, and he rewarded her by wiggling his backside. The giggle that bubbled up in her died as he disappeared into the bathroom.

Her reprieve from the truth had come to an end. She would have to talk to him, have to confess her lies as soon as possible, before she lost her nerve.

It wasn't what she wanted, but, then, getting what she wanted wasn't a possibility now. In a perfect world she could take up Ramsey's isolation with him, hide in this house forever, safe within the four walls of Kinross House and the strong, loving arms of the man standing in the shower.

She wanted to run to her room, to avoid talking to him altogether, but she knew if she ran she might as well keep running. So, she forced herself to lie there, imagining all the horrible things that might come from her admission, and waited for the shower to stop.

By the time it did she was all but chewing her fingernails.

Dressed only in his dark trousers, he appeared in the doorway. He padded toward her on bare feet, smoothing his wet hair back into a ponytail.

"I need a haircut," he said, flopping down on the bed.

"No, you don't," she said. She almost wished he weren't so happy.

He smiled at her, making the kind of light conversation normal couples have in the morning and, as a result, making it hard for her to tell him the truth.

"You don't think?" he said, squeezing a little cold water out of his hair onto her naked shoulder.

She flinched and stared at him absently.

"What's wrong, honey?"

Oh, God, he'd called her honey.

"I think we need to have a serious talk," Landis started.

"If you like my hair, I'll leave it long," he said.

"It's not your hair. I want to tell you about me. There are things you don't know."

"I know you're ticklish," he said. "I know you like your feet rubbed and that you purr like a kitten when I..."

"Ramsey, stop!" she said, too sharply.

He did stop and looked at her with those eyes that even now she couldn't read.

"Am I trying too hard?" he asked softly, the warm silk of his voice melting her heart.

"No," she whispered. "I'm...I'm..."

"You're trembling." He put his arms around her. "Landis, whatever you want to say, just say it."

"That's just it," she said. "I don't want to." Tears burned behind her eyes and clogged her throat, threatening to strangle her. But she had to keep talking. "I didn't tell you the truth about where I used to work," she said around the lump in her throat.

"You want to tell me you lied on your resume." He smiled. "I already know."

Landis choked on a gasp. "What? How did you know?"

"I've had personal secretaries before. And, honey, you're not very good at it. What did you do at the insurance agency? Receptionist? Clerk-typist? I told you before you're not a very good liar."

For a moment Landis lay very still, stunned. Her brain worked furiously to process what he had said. He had seen through some of her ruse, but he still didn't know all of it. He had no idea how deep her lies went.

She wanted to scream, to roll over on her stomach and have a good old-fashioned crying jag. Instead, she moved out of his arms and sat on the end of the bed.

"It doesn't matter to me," he said then, caressing her shoulder. He rose up onto his knees next to her, trying to reassure her, but it only made her feel worse. She just couldn't make herself tell him. If only he didn't look at her with such love—if he didn't try so hard to make things right—if she thought for one second her words wouldn't cut him to the bone...But they would, and in the end she was a coward.

"I don't care what you did before you came here." He kissed her neck. "All that matters is that you're here now."

"I wish I could believe that," she whispered.

"Go get a shower, get dressed, and we'll have a huge breakfast. I could eat a city bus. I tried to call Bridget earlier, but the phones are out from the storm."

"Ramsey," Landis said, gathering her discarded nightgown and robe. "You really wouldn't care what I did before?"

"Honey," he said with a devilish smile, "I'm the last person in the world who has the right to judge you. Go on. Before I think of something to keep you in my bed until noon."

Landis closed the door that led to the office and hurried through to her bedroom. It was a wonderful thought that he wouldn't care about the lies and what she had done to get close to him. But she knew it wasn't true.

All she had done was chicken out, and his words didn't change anything.

She still had to tell him the truth. But she didn't have to tell him right now. The phones were out and that meant she didn't have to worry about Paula for a while. For a while, she could just hold on to him a little longer.

~ * ~

By the time Ramsey and Landis entered the kitchen for breakfast it was well past nine. And despite doing their best to look cool and detached, Landis knew they were not fooling anyone.

The keen-eyed cook smiled at them as they ate, and Orphy, who breezed in from the garden, declared it was one of the most breathtaking mornings of the summer and suggested that Ramsey and Landis play hooky and spend the day at the pool.

Ramsey waited for Ivy and Orphy to leave earshot before he leaned toward Landis and whispered, "What do you think? The phones could be out all day, and I can't do anything else to the blueprints until I speak to Bridget. Unless, of course, you would rather spend the day locked in my room."

She was tempted. *It was all a fantasy*, the conscience that had niggled at her since her arrival at Kinross House reminded her. Then I'm going to live it to its fullest, she thought. "How about the pool and then your room?"

Ramsey slid away from the table. "Ivy, we'll have lunch out at the pool at one. In the meantime, find Eberhart and ask her if I own a pair of swimming trunks."

"Aye-aye," she said, saluting.

As the door closed behind them, Orphy turned to Ivy and gave her a high-five.

~ * ~

Landis stretched her legs out on the lounger and sighed contentedly. The sky was a perfect blue, unmarked by clouds. The hills that bordered the valley were emerald and jade, and for just a moment Landis let herself pretend life was as idyllic as the surroundings.

She watched Ramsey slice through the water. His hair streamed out like a dark cloud in the water, and his skin glistened. He broke the surface a few feet from her and locked his arms over the side of the pool, the muscles straining as he returned her heated gaze.

"I wish I had planted the backyard full of trees so those two spies in the house couldn't stand at the window and watch us," Ramsey said, lifting himself effortlessly onto the deck.

"Do you really think that's what they're doing?" Landis asked doubtfully.

"Of course." He shook his head, and tiny drops of cool water danced over Landis's skin. "Orphy keeps an antique spyglass in the library desk. She says it's for watching birds."

Eberhart had found a pair of swimming trunks for Ramsey, though she had huffed that they were barely decent. And for the first time Landis thought she might agree with the housekeeper. They were brief—very brief—and left nothing to the imagination. Landis liked them.

"If I thought for one moment they weren't watching us," Ramsey said with a wicked grin. "I would stretch you out on that recliner and make love to you right here."

Landis couldn't suppress a smile and a warm blush. Who would have thought that *the* Ramsey Cain, reserved recluse and social pariah, would say such a thing to her?

Instead of making good his threat, Ramsey stretched out on the lounger next to her, turned his face to the sun and closed his eyes. "I wish today could go on forever."

A sharp stab pierced Landis's heart. She wanted that, too. *No*, she told herself, *don't think, just enjoy.* "So if we weren't being watched, what would you do?" she asked, rising up on one elbow.

Ramsey's mouth curved into a seductive smile, but he didn't open his eyes. "Well, I would start by kissing the nape of your neck. Then taste the little hollow under your ear. That makes you shiver, you know. Your cheeks and eyes and nose. And then your mouth. I would untie that bathing suit top and let it drop to the patio. I want to see those perfect breasts in the sunshine."

A flush heated her cheeks. He described her breasts in such detail, as though he had studied every dimple and peak. She closed her eyes and let the images he described dance in her head.

"And your stomach—it's firm but soft, as a woman's should be." His voice was low and raspy, adding to the heat his words created in her. "I would run my hands over it and down until I found your..."

"My bathing suit is in the way," Landis said huskily and lay back on the chaise.

"Damn thing," he said. "I would tear it off your body. I want nothing between us. Then I would part your legs..."

"What about your suit?"

"It melted," he said, and Landis laughed at his impatient tone. "Now, hush."

~ * ~

In the library window, Orphy gave Ivy a nudge. "Come on, hand them back now."

Ivy passed the old nautical glass back to Orphy but continued to squint out the window. "I wish I were that robin sitting on the little table out yonder. What do you think they're talking about?"

"I think they're talking dirty to each other," Orphy said with a girlish giggle.

"Good heavens, what makes you say that?"

Orphy lowered the glass and grinned at her partner in crime. "Because those togs he's wearing don't leave a man much room to maneuver."

Ivy blushed to the roots of her hair. "Miss Orphy, the things you say."

Orphy smirked, then raised the glass to her eye again.

~ * ~

Dinner that evening was a celebration, Orphy was back to her lively self, Ivy McCreary's larders were full to capacity, and everyone knew, for the first time in distant memory, that the master of the house was happy.

A face once clouded with shadows was now quick to smile, shoulders once slumped beneath a burden too great were square and broad, and his attitude of darkness and mystery had given way to a proud strength.

Ramsey Cain was back.

He took the seat at the head of the table, his aunt on his left and Landis on his right. When he lifted his glass in salute to them both, he looked like a king.

Landis lingered over her glass of wine when dinner was finished and watched as Ramsey escorted his aunt to her bedroom. When her glass was empty, she started up the stairs herself.

But as she reached the landing at the top, a cold rush of air swept over her feet. She glanced down—and saw a sight that froze her heart in her chest and her feet to the ancient carpet.

The foyer seemed to fill with a gray-white mist, its cold fingers reaching up to wind around her ankles and wrap around her legs. In the midst of that damp fog a shimmering light gathered. The light became a figure, and the figure slowly became a woman.

She was dressed in a pale gown that clung to her generous curves. Her dark hair was styled up on her head and her face was cold and perfect. Landis knew that face; she had seen it many times on the news, in her dossiers, and in the wedding photos scattered around the library.

It was Holly.

The cold mist climbed Landis's legs, but it was the stern face of the entity in the foyer that made her shiver.

"Leave this house."

The words seemed to come from everywhere, and the voice was cold with fury.

She stared at the apparition. It couldn't be a ghost, her rational mind insisted. It had to be some kind of trick, a horrible joke. But the figure turned its attention up the stairs, seeming to lock its gaze with hers, and Landis fought a moment of pure panic. Then, though she couldn't quite put her finger on what it was, something made the panic abate. Something about this ethereal visitor wasn't right.

She didn't have the time to figure it out. Out of the darkness at the top of the stairs someone grabbed her. Landis screamed as a pair of strong hands wrestled her toward the stairs. She fought, trying to turn toward him—she was certain it was a man. A man trying to throw her down the stairs!

He pushed her, forcing her backward. She had to take a step, and she felt the edge of the top step beneath her feet. But she also managed to catch hold of her attacker. She felt a surprising strength in those thin arms. Beneath her grip the attacker's sleeve slid up, baring an arm covered with coarse hair.

She screamed again, but it was too late. She toppled backward.

~ * ~

Ramsey heard the scream. He dropped the jacket he had just put on a hanger and was already out the door when he heard it again.

Landis!

Reaching the top of the stairs, he saw the last fingers of pale mist evaporating; then, he saw Landis's unconscious form halfway down the stairs, her arm wrapped around a baluster. He called her name as he hurried to her and lifted her into his arms.

"He's getting away," Landis whispered.

"What happened?" Ramsey cradled her against him. Had she fainted? Had she seen Holly?

"Someone tried to throw me down the stairs," she replied weakly, trying to sit up.

"Don't move," Ramsey whispered, brushing her hair from her eyes. "You're safe."

Orphy's frightened face appeared at the top of the stairs.

"Call 911," Ramsey shouted up to her. "Get the police here."

"I was coming up the stairs," Landis said, leaning into Ramsey's embrace. "I saw something in the foyer." She lifted her gaze to his. How could she tell him she had seen his dead wife standing at the foot of the stairs?

"I know what you saw," he said softly. "What happened next?"

"Someone grabbed me," she said, watching the anger bloom on his features.

"You said 'he.' Are you certain it was a man?" he asked. "Could it have been—?"

"I'm sure. And he was flesh and blood. I felt his arms," Landis insisted. She tried again to get up. A wave of nausea washed over her, and behind her eyes pain began to beat against her temples. She lifted her hand and for the first time they both noticed blood staining her fingertips.

"Orphy, call an ambulance, too," Ramsey shouted.

"No, look," Landis said, wiping the blood from her hands. "It isn't mine. I must have scratched him."

Blood smeared her hands, but she wasn't cut and her hands didn't hurt. She wished she could say the same for her head and her arm. Both throbbed. "Why would someone want to hurt me?" she asked.

He took a damp towel from Orphy and gently wiped the blood from Landis's hands. "Perhaps it was a break-in."

"The police are on their way," Orphy said.

By the time police cars pulled into the drive Ivy had made a pot of tea, and Eberhart met the county detectives at the door.

"Detectives Musser and Shaw, Mr. Cain," Eberhart announced, leading the officers into the library. Ramsey had carried Landis to the sofa and sat holding her in his arms.

"Someone called in that a woman had been thrown down the stairs," the older of the two plainclothes detectives said with a smirk. "It was like that—what do they call it—deja vu."

"Believe me, Musser," Ramsey said, glaring at the officer. "I had hoped I would never see you again."

"Feeling's mutual, Cain," the cop said. "So, why am I here?"

"Someone attacked my...assistant," Ramsey said.

The younger of the two officers took a notebook from his pocket and made notes. "Did you get a look at him, Miss...?"

"Delaney," she said, sitting up a little straighter. "Landis Delaney. No, I was distracted by something and didn't see him until he grabbed me."

"Did he say anything?" the one called Musser asked.

"Nothing."

"How did you know it was a man?" Shaw asked.

"I could tell," she said, covering her eyes with her hand. Her head thumped. Shifting her focus from one detective to the other only aggravated it.

"Could you tell anything else about him? Was he tall, short, heavy, thin? Was he wearing cologne?"

"Can't these questions wait until the paramedics have a chance to check her out?" Ramsey asked, tightening his hold on her.

"Is there some reason you don't want us to talk to the young lady?" Musser asked.

Ramsey came off of the sofa, but whatever he intended to say was lost as the ambulance attendants entered the library. Landis thought it just as well. She didn't like the way the police had begun to look at him.

An efficient female ambulance attendant confirmed that Landis had taken a nasty fall but assured her that her headache was not the result of a concussion. Her arm was sprained but had no breaks. She also examined Landis's hands and confirmed that the blood was not hers.

She suggested rest and a trip to the family doctor in the morning.

"I'll want the towel you used to clean off the blood," Musser said, and Ramsey turned to Eberhart, who looked surprised.

"I threw the towel in the washing machine, sir," she said, wide-eyed. "I was afraid it would stain."

The cops exchanged a look, and Musser shook his grizzled head. "With that blood sample we could have ruled you out as a suspect, Cain. As it is—I think you better come with us to the station where we can talk."

"It wasn't Ramsey," Landis said. The painkiller the EMT had given her began to take effect, and, with the pain gone, her cloudy head had cleared.

Detective Shaw turned his attention to her.

"The man who grabbed me was tall, but very thin. He was strong, but..." she couldn't think of the word.

"Wiry?" Shaw offered and received a scowl from his partner.

"Yes," Landis agreed. "Wiry."

Landis noticed that Ramsey and Musser glowered at each other and decided that ending the interview would benefit everyone. "If that's all, those pills are making me a little tired."

Shaw closed his notebook and gave Landis a small smile. "We'll check out the house and grounds, but I think the excitement is probably over for the night. Come on, Phil."

Detective Phil Musser continued to exchange glares with Ramsey until they started for the door. Before stepping out onto the portico Musser caught the door and turned. "I never bought that story you fed to the coroner's office. The district attorney might not have wanted to take on the great and powerful Cain family, but I want you to know I'm still watching you, Cain."

Ramsey shrugged. "Yeah, well, I'm still innocent." He closed the door and came to Landis, concern and worry etched in the hard lines of his face. He put an arm around her shoulder and led her up the stairs.

She leaned against his strength and wished with all her heart she could just go to bed and rest.

~ * ~

Later, when the house was again quiet, Ramsey opened the door to Landis's room. This time he didn't have to walk cautiously. This time, he hoped she would be awake and waiting for him.

She turned on her pillow when the door opened and despite her heavy heart smiled at him. Silhouetted in the door frame, he paused, and Landis got an eerie sense of familiarity.

"You've come into my room before at night," she said softly. "Haven't you?"

He said nothing, but crossed to the four-poster bed that was a far cry from the polished contemporary one they had shared in his room.

"This bed was my parents'," he said, that soft rumble stirring her blood. "It suits you."

Landis knew he wasn't going to answer her question, but it didn't matter. She had secrets, and if he wished to keep one she didn't see the harm in that. She drew back the soft cotton sheets and light quilt, silently offering him a place. Ramsey slid in next to her, gathered her gently in his arms, and held her tight.

"How did I live without you?" he whispered.

She kissed him. The feel of his mouth on hers washed away the worry and drowned out her screaming conscience.

"I waited as long as I could," he said when the kiss ended. "Why didn't you come to my room?"

"I wasn't sure you wanted—"

"Of course, I wanted you to come," he said, holding her closer. "In case you've mistaken my intentions, I want you next to me, in my bed, in my life. I want to know that you're safe. Always."

"Are you certain?" she asked, clutching desperately to his words. "Because if you're not, please don't say it. I—I..."

"You what?" he asked, raising her chin to look into her eyes.

"I love you," she said.

How could three small words hold such power? Landis wondered. The moment they were out she felt her world rock, as though somewhere very near a bomb had fallen. And now she would have another mess to deal with.

He cupped her chin, his gaze holding hers captive. A smile curved the corners of his mouth. "I love you, too," he said, the heated velvet of his tone seeping into every pore of her body, easing the ache in her head and in her soul.

She wanted to hold the moment, to keep it next to her heart for a while. She wanted to believe that everything was all right. Tomorrow, she told herself, tomorrow she would tell him about the car brakes, and Paula, and all the rest. But tonight she wanted to lie in his arms, to draw his love around her like a warm quilt and sleep.

Ramsey kissed her and touched her and held her, and through the night with slow kisses and gentle caresses they proved to each other the depth of their love.

Thirteen

Morning came too soon. Though she woke to an empty bed, Landis had a moment of pure bliss. Then a tiny sliver of worry snaked its way through her.

Beyond the office door, she heard Ramsey talking to someone in a voice too loud. She shot out of bed and grabbed her robe, the quick action causing her head to thump. Stuffing her aching arms into the sleeves, she hurried across the room and tore open the office door.

Ramsey paced the floor, running his fingers through his long, dark hair. "This is such a crock," he snapped.

Landis flew across the room, ready to tear the phone from his hands if she had to.

"I didn't swear at you, Bridget," he insisted, and Landis nearly crumpled to the floor in relief.

"Tell George that the new heating specs have to be finished by the end of the week," Ramsey continued, and Landis lowered herself onto the chair at the drafting table.

As he spoke to his partner, Ramsey came to stand beside her. He brushed his knuckles over her cheek and wove his fingers into her hair. When Landis finally found the strength to look at him, he smiled and gave her a wink before turning his attention back to Bridget.

When the phone call ended, Ramsey again faced Landis, concern in his eyes. "You look pale, honey. Maybe you should see a doctor this morning, just to be sure you're all right."

"I'm fine," she said a little too breathlessly.

"Well, the phone is working," he said, holding it out for her. When she said nothing, he continued. "Did you want to call the garage about your car?"

"Not right now." Landis wanted to stand up, to step into the warmth and safety of his arms, but her legs shook and she didn't trust them to support her. "We need to talk."

Ramsey's smile weakened her resistance.

"I can think of better things than talking," he said in velvet tones that sent a shiver through her system. He reached for her hand, and Landis wanted to give it, but she knew time was running out.

"Please, listen to me," she insisted.

Ramsey moved the chair from his desk to sit facing her. He was listening, not making her laugh or charming her. All Landis had to do now was find a place to begin. The resume, the lies, the blackmail—no place seemed to be the right place.

Taking a deep breath, she began. "You said you knew I hadn't been a secretary before..."

"Honey, if this is about your resume—"

"No," she said before she let him stop her. "The resume is only a part of it. You were right. I wasn't a secretary, and I never worked for Northfield Insurance."

"Northeastern," he corrected. The expression he wore was one of growing confusion. "Northeastern Insurance."

"See, I can't even keep the lies straight anymore." She wanted to cry; her throat burned with the effort to hold the tears in check and just keep going. "I never worked for any insurance office. I wasn't a receptionist or a clerk. I was a researcher."

His brows knit and his eyes narrowed. "Researcher?"

Landis sighed and opened her mouth to continue when the phone rang again.

"I'm expecting Bridget to call back," he said, coming to his feet, the gentle satin gone from his voice, and picked up the phone. "Stay there."

Landis didn't move. Not that she'd have had the strength to go anywhere.

"What?" Ramsey said after a cursory hello. "How the hell did you get this—I told you a year ago I never wanted to hear your voice again... You have nothing to say that I want to hear, Paula!"

Landis moaned and covered her face with trembling hands. The wave of panic that washed over her nearly knocked her out of the chair. Faced with that fear, she didn't lunge for the phone as she thought she would; instead, she watched in horror as the color drained from Ramsey's face. After a long pause, he turned off the phone and dropped it onto the table.

The trembling had spread from her hands to her entire body. Her heart fluttered in her chest like that of a trapped bird.

Ramsey turned his back to her and crossed to the window. The way he always did when confronted with something he didn't want to face, Landis thought.

"Ramsey." Her voice sounded tiny and frail in the silent room.

"What could you possibly say to me?" he asked. His voice was as distant and cold as the fog that had filled the foyer the night before.

Landis fought to hold her tears in check. If she started to cry now she was certain she would never stop. "I need to explain."

"I think your employer explained it well enough," he said, keeping his back to her.

"Won't you let me tell my side of it?" Landis finally found the strength to come out of her chair. She took a step toward him, but he turned slightly and stopped her with an angry glance.

"Is there any difference in your version? You work for Channel Seven News, on assignment for *Pittsburgh Undercover*, for Paula Rice, and because of you my financial status will be their top story tomorrow night."

Landis groaned. Why hadn't she known that Paula would do this? Why hadn't she listened to her logic just this once and told him everything when she'd had the chance?

"So, if you have nothing more to add, I'll call you a taxi. I want you out of my house within the hour."

"Ramsey, please listen to—"

"More lies!" he shouted, turning to face her.

The fury in his voice made Landis flinch. She couldn't have imagined Ramsey so angry. His eyes were like a stormy sea, gray and cold. His face was dark, a mask of hurt and betrayal.

"No, " she said, trying not to sound broken. "I want to tell you the truth."

He threw back his head and laughed, a cold, ugly sound that chilled her to the bone. "The truth. That's very funny, coming from you."

Anger welled up inside her, anger at Paula and at Ramsey for not letting her explain. She raised her voice. "Did Paula tell you she blackmailed me into coming here? Did she tell you I didn't want to do this job in the first place? Or that I never wanted to be involved in this whole ugly business?"

Some of his anger seemed to leave him; at least that awful look of feigned amusement disappeared from his face.

"No, she didn't, did she?" Landis pressed. "Did she tell you I fought it, that I wouldn't have done it at all if she hadn't threatened to take my job from me? Did she tell you I quit that job yesterday rather than give her information on you or your family?"

"You told her Cain-Dunham was in trouble," he said sharply.

"I had to tell her something. She pressured me to come up with something scandalous. And all I told her was that you had a minor financial problem. She filled in the rest. I didn't think she would do a report on that." Landis covered her face with her hands and ran her fingers through her hair in frustration. "Ramsey, I knew the moment I walked into this house that nothing was the way I thought it would be. Orphy was so sweet to me; I didn't want to hurt her. And you...you were not the man I thought you were."

"Well, thank you for that, at least. I didn't turn out to be the monster that threw his wife down the stairs, just a lunatic who made the mistake of trusting you."

"I tried to protect you—"

"Protect me!" he shouted. "When those lawyers find out I'm nearly bankrupt, they'll pull out of the mall project. I'll lose everything!"

"I didn't know that would happen!" she shouted. "I just wanted to protect you from a personal attack. Paula tried to force me to come up with something else. She said no one was interested in your financial situation. She wanted me to say you were a drunk or that you used drugs. She wanted details about your love life—"

"Did she get them?"

It took a few minutes for the anger to abate long enough for her to answer. "She guessed we were lovers. But I didn't tell her how I feel about you."

"If I know Paula she won't be content to stop with my financial business if she can pin a sex scandal on me. So, brace yourself, you're about to become famous. Don't worry; she'll come up with something good, like your being the monster's sex toy or something. It'll make your family very proud of you."

"I was trying to buy time."

"For what?"

Four long strides brought him to her, but the warmth that usually washed over her when he was near was gone. In its place was only cold fury and betrayal that filled Landis with dread.

"Did Paula tell *you* she tried this before?" he asked. "That she tried to wheedle her way into my life herself?"

That revelation stunned her. Paula had always spoken Ramsey's name with such contempt. But Landis knew anything was possible with Paula.

"After Holly died, Paula offered all sorts of things," Ramsey snapped. "A sympathetic ear, carnal comfort. There was nothing she wouldn't do...for an exclusive. I told her to go to hell, and she swore she'd get me. She certainly found a way to do that, didn't she? She sent me something I couldn't resist. My very own Trojan Horse. Just go, Landis."

"I'll go. But first I have to tell you about the accident. My car—"

"I don't want to hear anything from you," he said.

Looking up into his hard face, she felt the first tear slip over her lashes and escape down her cheek. She had done the one thing she didn't want to do. She had hurt him, more deeply than she thought possible. When he looked at her now all the love and tenderness were gone. Even the cool, domineering man who had bantered with her but had carefully kept her at an arm's length was gone. All that was left was a man so hurt by life that his very presence was like a black hole absorbing all the light and warmth around him and giving nothing back.

And it was all her fault. It brought her tears in full force.

Ramsey grabbed her by the shoulders, shaking her sharply. "Don't you dare cry," he snapped.

The strong grip of his fingers on her arms did stop her tears, and for just a second Landis was frightened. Ramsey must have seen that fear in her eyes because he released her immediately.

"I want you out of my house," he said in a steady, controlled voice. "But first, I have one more question. Did Paula tell you to make me love you, or was that your own idea?"

He pushed past her and, crossing the room, flung open the door and shouted for Eberhart. His voice was a roar that echoed through the cavernous house.

The housekeeper appeared almost instantly, and Landis dried her face. She didn't want this woman to see her pain.

"Sir?" Eberhart said, looking from her boss to Landis and back.

"Get a taxi up here," he snapped. "Miss Delaney is leaving us."

Eberhart bobbed her head but said nothing. Landis thought she saw a satisfied smirk on the old housekeeper's face as Eberhart hurried out of the room, nearly colliding with Orphy.

"What's all the ruckus about? I heard you bellowing all the way to down in the kitchen," Orphy said, her hands on her hips.

"Landis is leaving," Ramsey explained, turning back to stare out the window.

"Leaving?" Orphy turned troubled eyes to Landis. "But I thought..."

"I have to go. Ramsey will tell you everything," Landis said, never taking her eyes off him.

Again the tears came. This time they poured unchecked over her cheeks, and she made a soft sniffing sound trying to hold them back. She wanted to throw herself at him, to beg and plead, and if she thought it would do any good, she might have done just that. But the Ramsey who had loved her was gone. In his place was a stranger who hated her and all she had done.

"I wasn't the only one who lied, Ramsey," she said around the sobs that clogged her throat. "You said it didn't matter what I did before. You said you loved me." Turning, she hurried from the room.

~ * ~

"Ramsey Duncan Cain," Orphy said sternly. "What's going on here?"

Ramsey didn't want to look at her. At that moment, he didn't want to look at anyone.

"What did you say to her?" Orphy asked, and when she realized he wasn't going to answer, she went into Landis's room and slammed the door behind her.

Ramsey thought his head might explode. He wanted to smash something, to hear the satisfying sound of something breaking. He wanted to hunt down Paula Rice and squeeze the life out of her.

What he did was stand at the window, the spot where he had first seen Landis, the sun glittering in her hair, where he had watched the way her hips swayed as she walked the long sidewalk to the house. Gritting his teeth, he prayed that he wouldn't go completely mad.

Orphy reappeared in the doorway. "She's really leaving Ramsey. She's packing her things and leaving you...forever. What the hell are you going to do about it?"

"I called her a cab." He kept his voice perfectly level, though inside he wanted to scream.

"Are you crazy?" Orphy grabbed his arm and wedged herself in front of him. "Have you truly lost your mind? You love her. She's the best thing that ever happened to you, and you're going to just let her walk out of your life forever?"

"Stay out of this," he warned softly.

"I will not—"

"Stay out of this!" he shouted.

Orphy straightened to her full five feet, four inches and gave him a hard stare. "If you let her go, you'll be making the biggest mistake of your life."

She turned and walked away, leaving Ramsey with a cold emptiness that he hadn't felt in weeks, not since a certain redhead had appeared on his doorstep. But it had all been a lie, and it was over now. Ramsey was left with just what he started with, a hollow place where his heart used to be and a ghost to remind him of who he was and what he was worth.

~ * ~

Melba Jackson set her cappuccino on her desk and took her seat at the computer. It was a little after five o'clock in the morning, and the station was still all but deserted. But that was the beauty of the information highway—it never closed.

She had tried every way she could think of to find something on Allison Eberhart. The night before, her husband had even suggested an actor's union might be one place to check, but when she got to work that morning she'd found a fax from Landis with the old woman's expired New York driver's license and Social Security card. It was all she needed.

She smiled as she tapped expertly into the New York State Department of Motor Vehicles database. It wasn't the most legal thing she had done all week, but it was hardly the most illegal. She told herself it was for a good cause.

"All right. Let's see," Melba said as she scanned the files available. "Eberhart, Albert...Allen...Allison."

Bingo! The listing was outdated but all she wanted was the last known address. From the DMV, she moved into the Social Security records. With the Social Security number she had no trouble locating a past employer, a small theater in New York that handled the garden variety of summer stock and off-off Broadway productions. But the last entry in the file made Melba choke on her coffee.

"That can't be right!" she exclaimed. She read the entry again, this time carefully taking in what it said, then downloaded the file and printed it out. As quickly as she could, she cruised through the offering of actor and acting-related web sites. As her husband had predicted, there was a site listing the stages' unions. She found the one most likely to list small theater and typed in Allison Eberhart's name. It was in the archive section that her name came up, and from there Melba found the file she wanted.

The photo was grainy but she could see it clearly enough to make out the woman's features. Allison Eberhart had round cheeks and a head of black hair that had to be one of the worst dye-jobs Melba had ever seen. But she had great eyes, wide and expressive.

Melba toggled down through the incredibly long list of professional credits. The woman had led a fascinating life. She had started out doing movie work back in the heyday of Joan Crawford and Bette Davis and had done the costuming for some of the biggest shows on Broadway, but the list ended in the early nineties.

Melba printed out the information and took down the phone number that had been included before she cleared the screen. She got an outside line on the phone and called the number provided in the information.

"Yes, this is...Paula Rice." No sense in sticking out her own neck. "From WALH-Channel Seven News in Pittsburgh. We're doing a feature piece on a local woman who worked for your theater. I was hoping you could give me some background on her. Her name is Allison Eberhart, and I believe she worked there until a few years ago. Any information would be useful... Yes. The theater will be covered as well. What was your name again? Is that with a 'y'? Of course, I can hold."

She tapped the tip of her pen on the desk as she waited.

"Yes, Miss Cory, do you have anything? I see... That's fascinating... Do you have a date for that? All right... no, you've been a great deal of help. I will send you notification if the story develops, of course. Thank you."

Melba dropped the phone onto the receiver and gathered all the papers from the printer. With the red pen she wore constantly behind her right ear she circled the item at the bottom of the file. Then she scribbled: "Confirmed by two sources. Good as gospel. A. M."

She convinced Jack Wilson to let her onto the research department's fax machine ahead of him. It cost her lunch, but it was worth it. The fax she sent to Landis was too important to wait.

~ * ~

Landis wasn't very careful about packing. She threw her few belongings into the suitcase along with the cell phone and the papers she had collected on Ramsey and the others. Ironically, those papers had seemed so important; now they meant nothing.

She went into the bathroom and with her newly formed habit closed the door behind her. She gathered her things from the shower, the medicine cabinet. She sat down on the closed toilet lid and stared at the bottle of shampoo in her hands. The thought struck her; she was really leaving. In a matter of hours she would be back in her little apartment on Highland Avenue. She would have to look for a new job, but, all-in-all, her life would probably go back to normal.

Normal? As if that were possible. Normal was lying in Ramsey's arms, listening to the heavy rhythm of his heart and the even sound of his breath. It was waking up and having breakfast and committing to him and having children with his sable hair and piercing gray eyes and growing old with him. Normal was the million everyday things that she would never get to do.

Sharp raps on the bathroom door made Landis jump and pulled her from the dreams swirling in her head, dreams she would never see come true.

"Landis?" Orphy called. "Are you all right?"

Landis opened the door and, stepping out, dropped her toiletries into her suitcase on the bed. "I'm fine," she lied and brushed a tear away before it dripped off her chin, but she could see from the old woman's sharp expression that she was having none of it.

"Well, you look like hell, my dear."

She hadn't thought Orphy would ever call her "my dear" again. The sound of it hit her like a trailer truck, and the tears came again. They burned in her throat and clogged her sinuses, then spilled like a torrent down her face.

"Oh, dear child," Orphy said, gathering her in her arms. "Come and sit with me a moment."

The old woman led her to the side of the bed and pushed a box of tissues into her hands.

Landis mopped at her face. "Is Ramsey all right?" She hiccupped gracelessly.

"Ramsey is stubborn and too proud by half, but I don't know if he's all right," his aunt said, a sad expression softening the lines on her face. "He won't talk, and I hate not knowing what has happened to rip the two of you apart. Won't you tell me what it is he thinks you've done that he can't forgive, and why did you say that you weren't the only one to lie?"

Landis took a deep, ragged breath and blew her nose. She knew she had to do it; she had to be the one to tell Orphy what she'd done because Ramsey wouldn't. His pride, his stubbornness wouldn't let him.

"I didn't tell him the truth," Landis said softly.

"The truth about what?"

"Who I am," Landis said, still trying to catch the tears that dropped from her eyelashes.

"You aren't Landis Delaney?" Orphy asked, trying to understand.

"Yes, but I lied about why I came here. I was blackmailed..."

Orphy gasped. "Who...? Why?"

"I work for a television station in the city, Channel Seven, or I did until yesterday. I quit rather than do the job I was sent here to do."

"What were you sent here to do?"

"I'm a researcher. Sometimes my department does research for *Pittsburgh Undercover*."

Orphy let out a low whistle and released Landis's hands.

"Paula Rice wanted to do a story on Ramsey and forced me to come here as his assistant to find out what he was doing and if he really killed Holly."

"Oh, my Lord." Orphy stood up, sighed, and paced the floor in front of Landis.

"I didn't want to do it..."

"She threatened to fire you?"

"Yes, " Landis said, hanging her head. "I never wanted to hurt anyone, not you, or Ivy, or least of all...him."

Orphy returned to her seat next to Landis and took her hands again. "I know that. And I'm sure you did everything you could to protect him. A researcher? You're not a reporter, then?"

"No. I'm a paper-pusher; I do facts and figures. Very clean, very anonymous. I'm no good at this spy stuff. Most of the time, I don't know what I'm suppose to do next."

Landis felt as though some of the burden had been lifted from her heart. Orphy did understand; and she didn't hate her—she could see that in the old woman's soft eyes and slow, sad smile. "But all Ramsey can see is that I lied to him. Orphy, what am I going to do?"

"You love him, don't you?" Orphy asked, her eyes narrowing as she studied Landis's face while she answered.

"Very much," Landis managed to say before a fresh onslaught of tears clogged her throat. "And I'm afraid for him. There's a lot more going on here than my spying."

"What do you mean?"

"That's the problem; I can't be sure but... I didn't tell you this before, but your accident wasn't an accident. The mechanic at the garage said the brake lines had been cut on my car. And that man on the stairs...that wasn't a burglary because nothing in the house was disturbed."

"Nothing but you." Orphy said. "Nothing like that had ever happened to you before?"

"No. I think it has more to do with Ramsey than me."

"Why would you think that?" Orphy asked, her brows furrowing.

"I've found other strange things since I arrived here," Landis confessed. "I was looking in Eberhart's room and found a date book belonging to Ramsey."

"In her room?"

"While I was snooping," Landis said sheepishly. "I found that date book that caused Ramsey to miss so many meetings and cost the company thousands of dollars in work stoppages.

"Oh, *that* date book," Orphy said shaking her head. "We turned this house upside down looking for that thing. Why would it have been in Eberhart's room?"

"I don't have an answer for that. But, then, I don't have a lot of answers when it comes to Eberhart. I had dossiers on all of you. The only person we couldn't find anything on was Eberhart. I needed her Social Security number so I broke into her room to look for it."

"Very clever of you, my dear," the old woman said with an admiring smile. "Did you find it?"

"Yes, and an old driver's license, and my friend Melba—Melba Jackson, she works with me in research—will be able to find out something from that."

"You think Eberhart is involved in some sort of plot against Ramsey?"

Landis hadn't really thought of it that way, but it was the only answer that made sense. No one had ever threatened her in her life, and certainly she hadn't wronged anyone badly enough to warrant two attempts on her life. Someone plotted against Ramsey, and hurting her would hurt him.

"If someone attacked me to hurt Ramsey, that means no one in the house is safe," Landis pointed out.

"We need to tell Ramsey about this," Orphy decided, wringing her hands nervously.

"Tell him what?" Landis asked. "We have no proof, and he wouldn't believe me now if I told him the sky was blue. No, we need evidence."

"You might not be a reporter, but you've ferreted out one lulu of a mystery. What do we do next?"

"What do you mean *we?*" Landis asked. "I just said this could be dangerous."

"I can't let you—"

"I've already made too many mistakes. I will not put you at any further risk," Landis said. "Just let me work on it when I get back to the city. I'm not sure what I'm going to do, but you have to promise me you'll stay out of it and stay close to Ramsey."

"I promise, but you have to promise *me* you'll come back. Ramsey may be angry, but eventually he'll realize his love is stronger than his anger. Now, I'm going to talk to Ivy. She's beside herself, and I'll bring you a pot of tea."

"My taxi will be coming soon," Landis said, shocked at how easily the pain returned and how bitter the words tasted in her mouth.

"Too bad," Orphy said with a wink. "Ramsey's paying for it. Let it sit in the driveway and idle for a while."

Orphy hurried out of the room, and Landis waited for the silence to descend again. The pain in her heart was like a living thing eating its way through her chest.

From the office a sound broke the quiet. The unmistakable clatter of the fax machine drew her to the doorway. She watched Ramsey's door on the other side of the room, hoping he would open it and cross to the machine.

But she knew it was wishful thinking. He wouldn't come out of the room, not until she was gone from the house once and for all. She walked slowly to the machine and lifted the first sheet of paper from the roller.

She saw a grainy photo of an old woman with jet-black hair and harsh make-up, but eyes that drew and held attention. Landis watched the second sheet come through—a file on Allison Eberhart from the Social Security office. She read each line as it printed, and caught her breath at the one word circled at the end of the file: *Deceased!*

"What?" Landis asked, as though the sheets of paper could answer her question.

The last of the message was written in Melba's familiar hand. *Confirmed by two sources. Good as gospel. A.M.*

Allison Eberhart was dead. It had to be a mistake. But when she checked the Social Security number against the one she had taken from *this* Eberhart's bedroom, they matched.

"So...if Allison has gone to that great theater in the sky, who the heck is dusting the dining room?"

There was only one way to find out.

She took the Social Security card and the fax with the real Eberhart's photo on it and opened the door into the hallway. She had to question Eberhart about her mysterious past, and, like it or not, she had to talk to Ramsey.

Fourteen

Beyond the office door, the empty hall and the house were silent. It was the same ominous silence that had filled Landis with dread a few minutes earlier. It was as though the house held its breath, waiting for disaster to strike.

She clutched the faxed papers tightly and hurried along the hall. Halfway down the great front stairs were Holly had met her untimely and unfortunate death Landis came face-to-face with the housekeeper. The woman shifted the tray of food she carried without so much as rattling the silverware and gave Landis a level look.

"Let me pass," Eberhart snapped.

"We have a few things to discuss," Landis said, standing her ground.

"I thought you were leaving," the woman answered, her voice cold.

The anger that bubbled up inside her took Landis by surprise. Who was this cool, unruffled creature, and what made her think she would get away with this ruse?

"Oh, I'm leaving," Landis assured her with equal coolness. She held up the photo of Allison Eberhart. "Just as soon as I talk to Ramsey about this poor woman."

The housekeeper's face went a deadly white. "Where did you get that?"

"Does that really matter?" Landis asked.

"No, I suppose it doesn't," she said softly.

Landis saw the tray tip and watched as the food slid precariously to one side. Eberhart, in front of her, moved with more speed than Landis could have imagined, snatching up the serrated-edged knife before the tray began to topple.

She lunged forward, grabbing Landis by the collar before she had time to muster a defense. The photo of Allison Eberhart and the other papers Landis had wanted to show Ramsey fluttered to the floor as she fought against the older woman's viselike grip.

She immediately knew she'd made a horrible mistake in not going to Ramsey first. This wasn't the thin, frail body of an aging domestic. It was strong, and *wiry*, and she had felt the strength of that arm before.

The thin material of the dress sleeve slid back under Landis's hand to reveal a clean white bandage, and she gasped. The man who had tried to throw her down the stairs would have a bandage over the scratches she had given him.

She tried to pull away, tried to turn and run back up the stairs, but the housekeeper pulled her against a hard, flat chest. Landis lashed out, arms flailing wildly for anything with which to fight back. She finally caught hold of the long gray braid that hung down Eberhart's back. It came off in her hand.

Immediately, Landis noticed the change in her attacker's face. The skin over the hard planes of the housekeeper's narrow face was rough and covered in a thick layer of outdated pancake make-up. It wasn't a woman's face at all. And Landis saw the knife held tightly in Eberhart's hand, poised to strike.

Eberhart turned her roughly, wrapped one strong arm around Landis's throat, and pressed the tip of the blade into her flesh.

"Damn you," Eberhart said, and even the voice was different. The timbre was richer, full, more masculine. "Damn you."

"Who are you?" Landis asked, struggling against his stranglehold.

"In good time," the imposter said. "I'm so disappointed. This is such a great shame. This is not at all as I intended things to turn out. I would've preferred your death to have more drama, more meaning; but as it is it will have to be quick and, of course, quick means messy. Poor Landis. Why couldn't you simply have gone away?"

Landis tried desperately to pull out of the man's grip and felt the bite of the knife's edge against her throat. "Why? I don't even know you."

"A thousand pardons," he said, pausing dramatically but not loosening his hold on her. "We were never formally introduced, were we? I am Edward Richards; Holly was my sister. Apropos, don't you think, that you will die by my hand the same way she died at his? A nasty fall down these very stairs. It's positively poetic."

He was insane. Landis heard the madness in his voice, in the almost gleeful way he described her pending death. He did intend to kill her, unless she did something to stop him.

He shifted Landis's weight and pushed her forward, forcing her back up the stairs. He intended to throw her down the stairs, just as he had tried to do the night before.

"You were the man here on the stairs last night!"

"Of course, my dear. But don't state the obvious. It makes you look less intelligent than you are." He snickered.

Landis leveled her foot against the next step, trying to push him backward. It surprised Edward. He pressed the knife again to the spot on her neck where the pulse hammered just beneath the skin, then pressed his mouth to her ear. "If you make a sound I'll slit your lovely throat. And I'd rather not make such a mess on my nice, clean carpet."

She tried desperately to turn out of his grasp, but the strength of his grip was too much and she managed only to pull herself away a fraction of an inch.

"Stop it," Edward said in a hoarse whisper, tightening his arm around her neck until tears sprang to her eyes. She couldn't breathe. She clawed at his arm. The knife bit into her neck, again stopping her struggles.

"If you had just gone away," Edward growled in her ear. "None of this would have been necessary."

He loosened his grasp and Landis gasped a breath. "Why...why did you try to kill me?"

"Once you gave yourself to him, I couldn't let you leave...unpunished. But at least your death will have meaning. The police will think our friend has been up to his old tricks again, that he killed you just as he killed my beautiful sister. I have nothing against you personally, you do understand that, don't you, Landis?"

"What about the ghost?" Landis asked, trying to buy so time.

Edward grew very still.

"I work with video. The ghost, Edward, it wasn't real, was it?" she pressed. "How did you do it?"

"You're a very bright little bunny, aren't you?" He sounded impressed. "You've figured out everything. Yes, I used the technology at hand to enhance the performance, but it never cheapened the experience. Every performance is a living, breathing thing. When Holly appeared to reap vengeance on that man, she was as real as you or me. And he certainly thought so. You should have heard him. *Why, Holly? You know the truth. Why do you haunt me?*"

The last he said in a theatrical whine.

"But how did you create such a performance?" She fought to control the conversation. Maybe if she could get him to loosen his grip she could get away. She knew she could appeal to his vanity, and he responded, smiling as though she had complimented him greatly.

"Oh, there are a hundred little gadgets one can use," he said, his tone relaxed. "This was a combination of liquid nitrogen to produce the fog, a fan for the cold breeze, and a small hand-held projection device I rigged in the library. I once used it to produce the ghost of Hamlet's father. I found a video of Holly. I believe it's called looping. I recorded one section of the tape over and over, then projected it onto the mist. Is your curiosity satisfied, dear Landis?"

Edward brushed a kiss on her ear.

The kiss was all it took to propel Landis to
She swung her arm, knocking the blade away

and pulled from his grip. She threw herself forward, scrambling for the knife.

Behind her, Edward lunged catching her ankle and dragging her backward. She screamed. He hit the side of her head with his fist. For a terrifying second, Landis thought she might pass out. Instead, she put voice to her terror and screamed again.

In a heartbeat he had her by the waist, and, too late, she saw the knife flash in his hand. It bit into her neck. At that moment a shadow fell across them from the top of the stairs. Both Landis and Edward froze.

Ramsey! Her heart cried out to him. If he was at all shocked or confused by what he saw, it didn't show in his cool gray eyes. He was in control, every bit the man with whom she'd fallen in love. He took the stairs two at a time.

Edward pressed the knife painfully into her throat. "Another step, and I'll kill her."

~ * ~

Those were the only words that could have stopped Ramsey. He was close enough to reach out and grab Landis, close enough to see the heavy make-up that smeared Eberhart's face and the rough complexion under that make-up.

"Who are you?" he asked.

"You haven't guessed? Of course, we've never met, and you had no reason to suspect that your trusted housekeeper might also be your brother-in-law."

"Edward," Ramsey growled in a low, hate-filled voice.

"I would say 'at your service,' but, then, I have been for quite some time. And you never suspected a thing," Edward taunted.

Ramsey glanced into Landis's face and saw the fear in her eyes. She was trying to be brave, trying not to panic, but she was very close to losing control. He had to do something, but the sharp blade of the knife at her throat made him cautious.

"It was very clever of you to hide right under my nose. Very clever," he said.

"I'm a clever man," Edward snapped.

"Give her to me, Edward," Ramsey said reasonably. "Your fight is with me, not Landis."

"The last woman I gave to you died," Edward said, his mouth twisting viciously. "I think I should keep this one. Let her die in my tender care instead of yours. Now, back up."

Without turning his attention from them, Ramsey backed to the top of the stairs, far enough to give them room on the landing.

"Very good, old boy," Edward said. "I promise you this last act will be the finest yet."

"I won't let you hurt her," Ramsey said again, and took a menacing step forward.

Landis surprised Edward by pulling away. It was all the opportunity Ramsey needed. He lunged forward, grabbing Edward by the collar of the old gray dress.

Edward turned and swung Landis in a wide arc toward the stairs. She stumbled, managing to avoid the steps, but hit the hallway wall. Her head struck the corner molding with a sickening thud.

Ramsey let go of Edward and made a dive for Landis, but Edward clipped him, sending him sprawling onto the landing. In a heartbeat he was on his feet and grabbed

Edward, driving the man back against the wall with a feral growl. Ramsey had underestimated the thin man's strength. He wouldn't make that mistake again.

Edward broke the hold and hit him a glancing blow to the jaw. Ramsey backed up a step. Edward lifted the oil lamp from the table.

The power had flickered several times since the storm, and the lamp had been left lit. Now, its flame wavered as Edward raised it high in the air and sent it sailing toward Ramsey. He dodged the missile but smelled the pungent scent of oil, and heard the whoosh of the fire as it exploded on the stairs behind him. Landis moaned softly. Ramsey's attention momentarily shifted from Edward to the woman sprawled unconscious on the floor. The flames began to spread up the stairs, over the rubber mat and old rose carpeting, inching slowly toward Landis.

"You won't escape," Ramsey said, hoping to buy the time he needed to get Landis to safety. "You're only risking your own life." He knew it was useless trying to reason with a madman, but he had to try, if only for her sake.

"Our business is not finished," Edward said, crouching low. "Holly will be avenged. You will die for killing my sister, and your whore will die with you."

He ran at Ramsey, but this time Ramsey was ready for him and hit him in the stomach, a blow that staggered the actor backward into the dark end of the hall. Ramsey hurried through the thick black smoke that rolled up the stairs toward Landis. He took her in his arms, lifting her as quickly as he could. He didn't get far before a shout rent the smoke-filled air.

Edward emerged from the cloud of smoke. Ramsey saw only a flash before Edward hit him with the small table that had once held the oil lamp. He dropped to his knees and staggered slightly, trying not to drop Landis. Edward lurched forward and wrapped cold hands around his throat.

He dropped Landis and struggled with the hands that strangled him. Despite the foul air and the strong grip the madman had on his windpipe, Ramsey managed to stagger to his feet. He jerked his head back, cracking Edward in the face.

Gasping for air, he choked on the smoke that now filled the hallway. The flames, fueled by the oil and the rubber mat, produced lethal fumes that quickly robbed his mind of clarity. The only blessing was, it hadn't affected only him. He heard Edward coughing and gagging from somewhere on the dark landing.

He glanced at Landis and noticed her lying in the few inches of breathable air that carpeted the hallway floor. He had no choice. Edward wouldn't let them out of the house, and if he lifted Landis from the floor he'd have only seconds before time would run out for both of them.

Without thinking, Ramsey dove into the thick cloud of noxious gas and found the air clearer on the east wing of the hall. He had to get Landis out of the house, had to save her.

He grabbed a startled Edward and hit him once, sending him sprawling back against the railing. The scene seemed to play out in slow motion. He advanced on Edward. The actor glanced over his shoulder and then back at Ramsey. He muttered a hoarse curse and tried to right himself. The rail cracked ominously, and, for a moment Edward pinwheeled his arms in a futile attempt to regain his balance. Ramsey lunged forward to catch him, but the rail splintered.

The remaining spindles looked like broken teeth opening to a fiery throat. With a bloodcurdling scream Edward toppled, falling backward into the smoke-filled foyer.

Ramsey leaned over the broken railing, but the flames had caught the woodwork at the bottom of the stairs and were licking the walls. Everywhere below was a sea of flames. There was no escape there.

He gathered Landis in his arms and carried her to the top of the old servant's stairs that led to the kitchen pantry on the first floor. That stairway had already begun to fill with smoke, but he could see well enough to make his way down. He bolted through the pantry door and into the kitchen and found it in flames.

He pulled Landis close, careful to keep her face pressed to his chest. His lungs burned, his head swam from a lack of oxygen, but he pushed forward. The new metal kitchen door was closed, and he hit it with as much force as he could muster. It didn't budge. In his arms Landis coughed and groaned while he struggled to shift her weight. He glanced over his shoulder.

The carpet in the dining room was a sea of fire, the flames licking greedily at the walls and spilling onto the new vinyl flooring in the kitchen. The fire had spread to the curtains and the small kitchen table. With grasping fingers outstretched it consumed everything in its path.

Ramsey managed to get a grip on the knob of the kitchen door and jerk it open. He tightened his arms around Landis and ran from the house. He made it as far as the grass beyond the flagstone walkway before a blast and rush of air caught him, hurling him forward into darkness.

~ * ~

The first thing Landis noticed was the sweet smell of fresh air. Breathing too deeply made her cough, but it also cleared her foggy head. She lay on her back, facing a clear blue sky that suddenly vanished in a thick cloud of black smoke when the fitful breeze blew over her. She slowly pulled herself up to a sitting position and blinked her eyes to focus them. Her head throbbed with each beat of her heart, and the pain blurred her vision.

The grass was burning to her left and to her right lay Ramsey, as still as death. His face was turned away from her, and it took a supreme effort to crawl to him.

"Ramsey, she said in a half-whisper, half-croak that couldn't have been heard above the roar of the flames. She called his name again, pulled herself closer, and sat up. She took his shoulders and, fighting a wave of nauseating pain, rolled him to his back and turned his face toward hers. A gash above his eye trickled a thin line of blood across his temple into his hair. She put his head in her lap, stroked his face, and repeated his name again and again.

Above the death throes of the house, Landis heard the sound of a siren and Orphy shouting her name, but she ignored it all. Nothing mattered but the man lying in her arms.

"Ramsey, please," she said in a sobbed whisper. "Please don't leave me."

His eyes opened slowly, and he tried to force a smile.

"Don't move," she said. "Help is coming." But the words were barely out of her mouth before Ramsey pulled himself up to sit next to her.

"My help is already here," he said, caressing her face. He gently brushed the hair from her eyes. "How did you know about Edward?"

"My friend, Melba, had been running a check on Eberhart..." A spasm of coughing over- took her. "She found out that the real Allison Eberhart died. The Eberhart we knew wasn't who she...he claimed to be." More coughing interrupted her. "I had to find out who she...he was. He told me he wanted revenge for Holly's death. It was all an elaborate plan to make you think you were going insane. Edward even stole the date book. I found it in a drawer in his bedroom."

"You *were* snooping," Ramsey said smiling.

"Maybe a little," she confessed.

"And the ghost?" Ramsey asked.

"It was a trick, the right lighting and a little video work...nothing more."

"In my state of mind, it was effective." He moved closer, stroking her arm with a hand blackened with soot. "I thought you could help me rescue my business. I never thought you would rescue *me*."

"I couldn't let you...I need to...I thought you hated me."

"I hated losing you," he said. Leaning forward, he took her face in his hands. "You must promise me you'll never leave."

"Even if you act like a madman?"

"Especially when I act like a madman."

"I promise," she said softly. "But do you forgive me...for the lies?"

Ramsey kissed her.

When his mouth left hers, she smiled. "I have to hear you say it. Do you forgive me?"

He lifted her face to meet his. "You are exasperating."

"I know, but do you forgive me?"

"I forgive you," he said, purposely dropping his voice to that tone that made her shiver. "I need you. I want you. I love you."

He kissed her again, a long deep promise that life would never be the same.

~ * ~

Orphy and Ivy led a frightened-looking Melba through the trees at the end of the yard. It had taken Melba an hour to get to the small town and now, despite Orphy's reassurance that Landis was fine, she had to see for herself. The fire department, however, wasn't letting anyone but the paramedics through while they worked to put out the last of the hot spots.

Both Ramsey and Landis had been treated at the scene for smoke inhalation and their minor injuries, and both had refused to go to the hospital. Ramsey refused to leave Kinross House as it passed away, and Landis refused to leave him. They stood under the huge maple to the right of the pool, their arms wrapped tightly around each other.

The fire chief approached them cautiously, as though he were unwilling to interrupt their silent vigil over the ruined house. "Mr. Cain," he said apologetically. "I'm Joe Baker with the Cherry Run Fire Department. The county coroner is waiting to talk to you. We...we found a body in the building."

"It's Edward Richards, my late wife's brother." Ramsey's voice sounded bone-weary, and Landis tightened her arms around his waist. "Will you need me to identify the body?"

The fireman looked embarrassed. "I'm afraid that wouldn't be possible. But there are two county detectives and a squadron of news vans out front. My men won't let anyone back here until you're ready."

Ramsey sighed heavily as Joe Baker walked away. "Musser. I suppose he'll find a way to pin this death on me, too."

"He can't," Landis said. "You have something now you didn't have the night Holly died."

He brushed a sooty curl from her face. "What's that, darling?"

"Me," she said, giving him a tired smile.

On the sidewalk, Ivy, Orphy, and Melba were too far away to hear what Ramsey and Landis said but they watched them embrace, and Ivy sniffled softly into a wad of tissues.

"Oh, for heaven's sake," Orphy chided. "Why are you crying?"

"Look at them," Ivy sniffed. "Despite it all, they're happy."

"I have a lot to tell her about the station," Melba said in a voice that quivered. She took a clean tissue when Ivy held one out to her.

"I think all that can wait," Orphy said, then let out an exasperated sigh as she looked at the openly sobbing Ivy. "You should save that for the wedding."

Orphy stopped to watch her nephew kiss the woman he loved. After a few moments she, too, snatched a tissue from Ivy's hand.

Epilogue

Landis's tiny apartment in Pittsburgh's Oakland neighborhood was a far cry from the grandeur of Kinross House, which, in Ramsey's opinion, made it the perfect spot for a honeymoon. They had spent two weeks hiding out, away from family and friends, surviving blissfully on leftover wedding food and passion.

The television provided the only light in the bedroom Landis described as decorated in early thrift shop. They had just finished watching the video tape of the wedding. A gift from her friends at the station, it was a beautifully edited and magnificently presented film that chronicled the start of Ramsey and Landis's life together, with commentaries by all the people who loved them both. Landis had cried at the sentiment behind Orphy's words of love and encouragement, then laughed when the camera caught her crying into her handkerchief at the ceremony.

When the tape finished, Landis turned off the VCR but left the television on. She spooned ice cream into her husband's mouth and kissed him, tasting the sweet rocky road on his mouth. The kiss became a seductive caress, and it wasn't hard for Landis to guess where it would lead.

She pulled away and smiled. "Did I tell you what happened at the station?"

"No," Ramsey said, rising up on his elbows.

"Melba said that management had the three-piece suits swarming over the station so fast Paula didn't have time to cover up her paper trail. Old man Peterman wanted to know why she had a copy of my contract in her desk. She had even highlighted the section on not fulfilling my duties. They also wanted to know why no one had been informed that I was working undercover. Paula claimed I was acting alone, but someone found a voucher Paula had filled out giving me the use of the cell phone. Can you believe it?"

"I said the woman was vicious; I never said she was bright." Ramsey leaned toward her to trail kisses into the soft flesh inside her elbow. He paused there to taste the warmth of her skin on his tongue.

"I'm trying to tell you what happened at the station and you're distracting me," she said, but her complaint sounded hollow and breathy.

"You have fifty years to tell me how it turns out," he answered, pressing her back onto the bed.

"Fifty years will never be enough time to get used to this." Landis reached behind her to set the empty ice cream bowl on the nightstand. The feel of his skin under her hands, the taste of his kiss, the depth of his passion, were things she knew she would never grow tired of.

Ramsey had slipped the thin nightgown over her head when a familiar music filled the room, and the opening credits of a local television program began.

"Good evening and welcome to Pittsburgh Undercover," the blond-haired anchorwoman said, smiling

sweetly. *"I'm Janice Elliot, sitting in for a vacationing Paula Rice. Tonight we start with a story out of Armstrong County. Last week, Ramsey Cain, millionaire recluse, lost his family home in a fire that claimed the life of his former brother-in-law, stage actor Edward Richards. You will remember that a year ago Cain was cleared in the death of his wife, socialite Holly Richards Cain. He has since lived in seclusion at Kinross House in Cherry Run.*

The camera did a close-up as Janice Elliot's smile widened. *"But hope blooms out of_tragedy as Cain recently married former Channel Seven staffer Landis Delaney. We here at Pittsburgh Undercover wish the happy couple well and hope this closes a dark chapter for the head of Cain-Dunham, the city's premier architecture firm."* The camera angle changed but Janice's smile remained brilliant. *"Next, does the Pittsburgh Police use a family of psychics to help solve some of its toughest crimes? And the latest on the Penguins' Stanley Cup hopes after these messages."*

Ramsey scrambled for the remote on the nightstand and, laughing, turned off the TV.

Meet Marcy Graham-Waldenville

Marcy Graham-Waldenville lives in Western Pennsylvania with her husband, Ken, her son, Jesse, and daughter, Sarah, and two loveable mutts, Dudley and Buffy. When she isn't spinning a tale about her two favorite things: romance and murder, she sells Amish made furniture and works to improve the century old farmhouse she calls home.